Kobzar's Children:

A Century of Untold Ukrainian Stories

Edited by
Marsha Forchuk Skrypuch

Fitzhenry & Whiteside

Copyright © 2006 by Marsha Forchuk Skrypuch

Published in Canada by Fitzhenry & Whiteside, 195 Allstate Parkway, Markham, Ontario L3R 4T8

Published in the United States by Fitzhenry & Whiteside, 311 Washington Street, Brighton, Massachusetts 02135

www.fitzhenry.ca   **godwit@fitzhenry.ca**

10 9 8 7 6 5 4 3 2 1

Library and Archives Canada Cataloguing in Publication

Kobzar's children : a century of stories by Ukrainians / edited by Marsha Forchuk Skrypuch.

ISBN 1-55041-954-4 (bound)
ISBN 1-55041-997-8 (pbk.)

1. Canadian literature (English)—Ukrainian-Canadian authors. 2. Ukrainian Canadians—History—Literary collections. 3. Canadian literature (English)—20th century. I. Skrypuch, Marsha Forchuk, 1954-

PS8235.U4K62 2006   C810.8'0891791   C2005-907258-X

U.S. Publisher Cataloging-in-Publication Data (Library of Congress Standards)

Skrypuch, Marsha Forchuk, 1954-
Kobzar's children : a century of stories by Ukrainians / edited by Marsha Forchuk Skrypuch.
[256] p. : cm.
Summary: An anthology of stories and poems that chronicle the lives and struggles of Ukrainian immigrants during the past century.
ISBN 1-55041-954-4
ISBN 1-55041-997-8 (pbk.)
1. Canadian literature (English)—Ukrainian-Canadian authors. 2. Ukrainian Canadians—History—Literary collections. 3. Canadian literature (English)—20th century. I. Title.
810.8/08 /917/91 dc22   PS8235.U4K62 2006

Fitzhenry & Whiteside acknowledges with thanks the Canada Council for the Arts, and the Ontario Arts Council for their support of our publishing program. We acknowledge the financial support of the Government of Canada through the Book Publishing Industry Development Program (BPIDP) for our publishing activities.

Design by Fortunato Design Inc., Toronto
Printed in Canada

Contents

Acknowledgements

This anthology would not have been possible without Gail Winskill, whose faith in this project made it a reality. Sincere thanks also to the Ukrainian Canadian Foundation of Taras Shevchenko; to Ann Featherstone for her patience and expertise; and to Fortunato Aglialoro for his beautiful design work.

Cover image: Library and Archives Canada.
Photo credits: all photos supplied by the authors with the exception of pp. vi, 144—Ed Pancoe; p. 17—from the documentary "Freedom Had a Price," Yurij Luhovy, associate producer/editor; pp. 31, 69—Leonard Krawchuk; p. 48— from the documentary "Harvest of Despair," Yurij Luhovy, associate producer/editor; p. 81—Oksana Kuryliw; p. 91—Angela Birt; p. 94—from *Into Auschwitz, For Ukraine*, Gerry Locklin and Lubomyr Luciuk, Kashtan Press; pp. 169, 187—Ruslan Tracz

Sonja Dunn's poems, "Memories of Volodymyr Serotiuk's Birthday," "Babyn Yar," "Veechnaya Pamyat," "Before Glasnost, Oy Tovarish," "Violin," and "The Gift" originally appeared in *Uncivilizing*, Insomniac Press, 1997. Reprinted by permission of the publisher.

Stefan Petelycky's story "Auschwitz: Many Circles of Hell" is excerpted from his memoir, *Into Auschwitz, for Ukraine*, Kashtan Press, 1999. Reprinted by permission of the publisher.

*(left to right) Josef Pankiw, Tanas Pankiw, Walter Pankiw (Pancoe),
and Domka Friend-Pankiw. Taken around 1914,
one year after arriving in Canada from Ukraine*

Preface

When I was a teen, I was an avid reader. I picked up all sorts of novels, short story collections, and memoirs; but I was never able to find stories about Ukrainians who had come to North America. My Ukrainian grandfather died when I was in grade eight, and my grandmother died when I was in grade ten. But my father is a wonderful storyteller, and he did tell me all sorts of stories that his parents had told him. He also told me stories of his own childhood.

I longed to read books about Ukrainian immigrants, but I could not find any. I know, now, that there were stories. But they were written in Ukrainian, and because I couldn't read or write Ukrainian, they were not accessible to me. One time, when I was about ten years old, I found a book about Cossacks in our local public library. It was the first and only time I found a story remotely about Ukrainians. I took that book home and read it cover to cover. I still remember the colorful illustrations of men with their tonsured hair flowing, riding their mighty horses across the Steppes. I took that book out of the library so often that it began to fall apart.

Because I couldn't read about Ukrainians, I decided to do the next best thing. I read Russian stories, Polish stories, and Jewish stories. The stories plunged me into a different time and place, and they were very moving; but I began to notice a disturbing trend. Ukrainians were often portrayed with negative stereotypes. I noticed the same when I read North American stories about Ukrainians. While it was frowned upon to stereotype other ethnic minorities, why was it acceptable, and common, to portray people whose names ended in *chuk, iuk, ski,* and *enko* as buffoons, bullies, drunks, and murderers?

It wasn't until I was an adult that I heard about the *kobzars.* These were the blind, wandering minstrels of Ukraine. The kobzars memorized long epic poems that had been passed down from generation to generation. These poems captured the rich history, the folk tales, and the cultural identity of Ukraine. When a kobzar came to a village, he was clothed and fed. And people gathered round to hear the tales.

During Stalin's regime, kobzars were people who could pass information from one village to the next. Now, the older tales were intermingled with contemporary stories of Soviet repression, famine, and terror. Stalin heard about these kobzars, and he was not amused. In the 1930s, he called the first national conference of kobzars in Ukraine. Hundreds congregated. And then Stalin had them all shot.

As the storytellers of Ukraine died, the stories died too. But Stalin wasn't content with this. He rounded up Ukrainian journalists, artists, novelists, and playwrights, and murdered them, too.

The word *kobzar* resonates for another reason. Kobzar is the title of Taras Shevchenko's first collection of poems, published in 1840. Taras Shevchenko was born a serf in Tsarist Russian-controlled Ukraine but rose to be Ukraine's most beloved poet and artist. He suffered censorship and exile in his lifetime for writing about the rich history and culture of Ukraine. He is popularly known as The Kobzar. During Stalin's time, Shevchenko's writings were deliberately falsified.

Some Ukrainians did escape the Stalin terror. And some of them immigrated to North America. But these immigrants were not writers. They were farmers, pharmacists, engineers, and coal miners. Even now, although there are millions of North Americans whose roots are in Ukraine, only a handful of them are writers. My passion is to write stories that capture real experiences that have been suppressed or lost. That's why I often write about Ukrainians. When you don't write your own stories, others will write their versions for you.

After I published a few books touching on Ukrainian history, people began to contact me by e-mail, telephone, and letter. *Thank you for writing my story,* one letter said. *It is time that the record has been set straight,* said another. Others wrote, *I have a story, too.* After a while, I gathered together people who had stories and started up a small e-mail critique group. It was through this group that most of the stories in this collection have emerged. They are arranged in chronological order, beginning with an early homesteader tale in 1905 and ending with a story set during the Orange Revolution and the election of Yushchenko in 2004.

We are the Kobzar's Children. Our parents and grandparents suffered in silence, with their life stories and histories either suppressed or falsified. This anthology tells a century of untold stories. I hope that after you read this book you will be inspired to talk to someone whose stories have been deliberately forgotten. The injustices that we forget, we are bound to repeat.

–MARSHA FORCHUK SKRYPUCH

A Home of Her Own

OLGA PRYCHODKO

This story is set in the early 1900s and is an excerpt from Waskatenau Girl, *a self-published memoir by the late Olga Prychodko. This story is about Olga's mother and her misconceptions about immigrating to the wilds of Canada's west.*

My mother, Emilia Makar, was twenty years old when she arrived in Lamont, Alberta, by a CN train on June 16, 1912.

She was the third of four children. Josefa and Hanka were her older sisters; and a brother, Stefan, was two years younger. They all attended the public school in their Ukrainian village. Josefa and Hanka completed school, but my mother dropped out after a couple of years. She enjoyed a more carefree existence. Throughout her entire life, her favorite occupation was helping around the house and garden. My mother's grandparents were Pavlo and Yeva Kulchycky. They were wealthy landowners and lived in a big brick house on the outskirts of Slovita. They also owned a couple of smaller houses that were used for the servants. Besides ten or twelve field workers, they employed two or three domestic servants, and a driver for the carriages. During a period of Polish repression, the Kulchyckys were forced to adopt the Roman Catholic religion and to declare themselves Polish in order to save the estate from expropriation.

1

During her childhood and adolescence, my mother loved to spend her time on the Slovita estate. She lived there more than in her own home. It was a happy time of her life. She was not prepared for a life of poverty and privation in Canada.

Many times, I heard my mother warmly reminisce about her happiness in Ukraine. She spoke of the merry gatherings of relatives at her grandfather's estate. They celebrated feast days, name days, engagements, weddings, christenings, and simple family visits. It was exciting to watch the guests arrive; everybody came, uncles, aunts, children, grandchildren, cousins, godparents, in-laws, the old, and the young. Visitors arrived from other villages. They arrived in carriages and stayed for days, feasting happily together. And when they departed, they left reluctantly until the next time, sad to leave their loved ones.

My mother was a lively, pretty child who was pampered by all her family. Her sisters were considerably older than she was; they were teenagers when she was born. She was especially attached to her brother. They were inseparable as children. And although they lived half a world apart, their strong bond lasted until his death in 1967. She was heartbroken at his passing.

In her youth, Emilia was the belle of the village. She was very popular and there was not a wedding where she was not a bridesmaid. She loved singing, and she would often sing as many as 200 songs during a wedding celebration. Most of her songs were sentimental wedding ballads based on tragic and interesting stories. And I learned years later that she had composed many of them herself.

Running home breathlessly from the field she would ask, "Mother, Mother, did they come to invite me?"

"Of course they came to invite you. Could there ever be a wedding held without you?"

Many young men sent matchmakers with proposals of marriage. Some of them were rich. The rich ones were much approved by her parents and grandparents, who had ambitious plans for her to marry well.

"Look, you're sixteen years old already," my mother said to me one day, "and nobody wants you. By the time I was sixteen I had a dozen proposals. Everybody wanted me." But she didn't want any of them.

She was waiting for word from Canada. Her fiancé, Andriy Harasimiw, had traveled to Canada in the spring of 1910. He had gone before her to carve out a new life for them on a homestead in the forests of northern Alberta. It was a dream come true when my mother's ticket finally arrived.

The first thing she did in preparation for her journey was to call her relatives and girlfriends together so that she could distribute her clothes. She didn't need them anymore, only those for travel. She was going to Canada, land of plenty. She would have the finest things, like those she saw in the stores in Lviv. My father had written from Canada that his entire farm was covered in thick forest. In her mind, according to the values in Ukraine, where only the well-to-do owned stands of woods, the trees on the Canadian farm represented great wealth.

The day of departure arrived and my mother had to say good-bye to Ukraine. She was accompanied by many relatives and driven, by team, from Slovita to the town of Hlyniany. From there she took a train to Lviv, changed trains, and continued to Antwerp, Belgium. She waited for a week for a boat to arrive and was housed with other emigrants in special emigration quarters. Their meals consisted mainly of beans, occasionally with some bread, and herring. My mother did not like the food and went hungry. Finally they boarded the ship, *Sofia Wisiadecka*, and started their arduous voyage to Halifax.

The rough crossing lasted twenty days. People became very sick. There were many stops and delays due to icebergs. At one point, the boat stopped for six days waiting for the icebergs to pass. Waves as high as mountains crashed against the boat. This was the year of the sinking of the *Titanic*. People were very apprehensive; some panicked.

On the twentieth day, the ship docked in Halifax and my mother boarded the train bound for Lamont, in Alberta, over 3000 miles away. After brief stops in Montreal and Winnipeg, where she received a proposal of marriage from one of many unattached homesteaders, she finally reached her destination. Besides the railroad station, Lamont now boasted a flour mill, a post office, a hotel, a small restaurant, a shoe repair shop, and a few small houses.

Having arrived in Lamont, my mother set out to find the home of a Mr. Rebus. He was the steamship agent who had arranged her trip. She had instructions from my father to go to Rebus' place and to wait for him there. She stayed with this family for three days before Mr. Zomnir, my father's uncle, came for her. Although my father knew the approximate date of her arrival, he didn't know it exactly. He and his uncle had taken turns in coming to Lamont to check with Mr. Rebus.

Immediately, she and Uncle Zomnir started walking north, out of Lamont. The trek to his farm was eighteen miles of winding trail through bush, swamp, and knee-deep mud puddles. After a few hours, they stopped to rest with some people that Uncle knew. They were welcomed warmly; invited to have dinner, and treated with enthusiastic hospitality, as if they had been relatives. Farther on along the way, my mother's now badly battered cardboard suitcase cracked open, and her belongings scattered over the wet ground. She gathered them up; tied a kerchief around the broken pieces of the suitcase, and continued. By nightfall, they reached Zomnir's farm. After supper, she fell asleep; but was soon awakened by a commotion outside:

"Is she here?" she heard, as the rumble of wagon and horses came to a halt.

"Yes, yes, she's here."

My father had come to ask his uncle about news from Lamont. One can only imagine what went through my mother's and father's hearts and minds as they embraced together after such an arduous journey and long period of separation.

Because there was no Ukrainian priest in the vicinity at that time, my parents, Andriy and Emilia, traveled about fifty miles by wagon to Fort Saskatchewan, where a French priest married them.

And so, my parents became part of the multitudes of Ukrainian pioneers who had been enticed by the Canadian government to come and build the West.

My mother's first experiences were traumatic. She suffered severe culture shock and, to the end of her days, never really reconciled herself to her extreme disappointment. She had expected to better her life in Canada; her lot became one of poverty, hard work, and hunger.

My parents lived in a little one-room hut with a *siny* (entry). There was a bed in one corner, a four-burner cast-iron wood stove in the other, a long table under the small window, and two benches along each side of the table. My father had made all the furniture by hand. On the bed lay a mattress, which was made from a large sack stuffed with hay, and a couple of rough gray blankets. The walls, inside and out, were plastered with clay. A couple of years later, they would be whitewashed with lime and would look white and bright. The roof was sod and the floor was smooth, hardened clay.

When I was about four years old, one of my daily chores was to sweep this floor with a handmade twig broom. Mother had taught me how to make a broom by cutting lengths of young, supple willow twigs, leaving some leaves at one end, and tying them all securely with twine. I swept toward the outside door, right through the entry, and over the threshold. The immediate area outside was also cleaned.

Everything had to be neat, and I liked to make it that way.

A myriad of flies would collect inside the house in the summer, and chasing them out was another unpleasant chore. The procedure was to hang sheets or blankets over the windows to make the room dark. Then, waving a leafy willow branch in each hand, I would start at the farthest corner and work toward the open door. The flies would be drawn to the light, and it was possible to shoo out whole clouds of them. Then I would go back for the stragglers. I used to pride myself on being able to chase them out, almost to the last one.

My mother whitewashed the walls of the hut regularly, inside and out. She used a lime solution and a brush made of fine straw or grass. She was especially careful to make it freshly white before all the feast days. In summer, the place shone brightly in the sun, like some kind of jewel in the surrounding wilderness. In winter, only the inside could be cleaned. But then, too, the sheer whiteness of the clean snow outside brightened the harsh existence somewhat. We couldn't afford store-bought pictures for the walls, of course, so we hung items at hand with pretty pictures on them, including a calendar from a mail order company and seed packages, along with two very imposing icons, in black frames which father had made and painted. Near the hut was a crude shelter for the horses.

By about 1918, after eight years in Canada, some progress had been made on the farm. There were three cows, three horses, a sow with a litter, and a couple more hogs that were waiting to be marketed. The yard swarmed with poultry, twenty or so chickens, a rooster, and five or six ducks. Between ten and fifteen acres of land had been cleared and cultivated. A team of horses now hauled wheat sheaves to a threshing machine that was owned by people a few miles away. Farming had become a full-time occupation. My father no longer went out for hire. There was even talk of building a new house.

My mother and father chose a location that was at the opposite corner of the property from where the old hut stood; the southwest corner instead of the northeast. It was on higher ground, and near what would become a main road. Road allowances had already been surveyed, and roads would be built later. In the meantime, people continued to travel along trails that wound through forests, and around bogs and sloughs and marshes.

In extremely wet places, impossible to circumvent, they built what they called terraces. These were simply piles of logs. They were thrown across the mud, so that the wagons could drive over without getting stuck. But often they did get stuck, and that was a calamity. Wheels sank up to the axles and horses, mired knee-deep, struggled, panted, and sweat. No amount of whipping, nor any amount of yelling and swearing, could prompt them to budge. They reared, and neighed, and snorted. Sometimes the wagon overturned and spilled store-bought staples, like flour or sugar, into the mud. Women, children, and babies panicked and cried when wagons became stuck. Only one remedy existed, to go for help, on foot, to the nearest farmer and bring back another team of horses. With four horses and much prodding and shouting, "Giddy-up, gee, haw, go, Sam. Go, Jim. Go, go," and with the men pushing the wagon from behind, the team that had been stuck would somehow clamber out onto dry ground.

For two or three years, building the new house was the main family project. Much attention and energy went into its planning and construction. The old hut had become practically uninhabitable. The sod roof was disintegrating fast because the snow and rain flushed the earth away. Muddy streaks leaked through the holes into the room below. The frame was crumbling, too. Cold drafts blew in through the cracks. A new house was an urgent necessity. But first, my father had to secure the building materials.

For two winters, Father cut logs in the bush around the towns of Newbrook and Boyle, about forty miles away. Winter, of course, was the only time during the year that he was not devoted to the never-ending labor of farming and improving the homestead. Although many trees grew right on the farm, they were mainly prairie poplars and aspen, which were not good for building because they were softwoods. For that reason, people went north for spruce and tamarack. Another reason these trips could only be made in winter was that the North Saskatchewan River was frozen over and passable. Newbrook and Boyle were on the other side of the river, and it was impossible to cross in summer.

Much preparation was required for these trips. The sleighs and the harnesses for the horses were checked and repaired. Saws, axes, and all sorts of other tools were assembled and examined. Clothes and horses' blankets were very important items. In minus-65°F weather, one could easily get frostbite or freeze to death. Food had to be prepared, as did hay for the horses. Getting logs involved a trek of many days, depending on how readily available the trees were, and how quickly it was possible to hew and trim them into suitable lengths.

My father selected the trees carefully and had to cut them precisely with a crosscut saw. The logs had to match in thickness and length, for they would be used for the main frame of the structure. The timbers were squared on two sides, so the walls would come out flush, both inside and out. When Father had collected a full load, he would return home to unload. He would take a few days off, to reorganize, before making another journey for more. Some logs were hauled to a sawmill, where they were processed into the boards, planks, and other materials that we needed for trim. My parents bought shingles at a lumber store.

In a couple of years, all was in readiness to begin actual construction. As was the custom, neighbors and friends came to

8

help. Whenever any family member was faced with some major undertaking or predicament, neighbors rallied. There was no mention of hiring, or payment, or bargaining for a return favor. It was a tradition that no longer exists. The community was one big family. People knew what each family was doing. For instance, everybody knew what progress was being made with plowing, harrowing, or tilling. People knew how much hay was already made, or how much harvesting was completed. Whenever people met or gathered, they invariably talked about their affairs:

"Fedko is ready to start seeding, but his horse sprained an ankle so I am lending him my brown one."

"Stefan has a few hogs to be castrated; let's go give him a hand."

"Ivan is digging a well; he could use some help."

Women, too, had their particular concerns: "Nastya's cow went dry and her children need milk. I'll take over a pail today; could you do it tomorrow and maybe Maria can give her some on Tuesday?"

"How long has Hanka been pregnant? She must be due to go into labor. Let's go help her get ready; maybe clean the house, or cook something."

"What are you doing today?"

"Where were you yesterday?"

"Is your young mare in foal?"

"Is your wife feeling better?"

"Are you going to Lamont soon?"

A universal problem was money, or the lack of it. There were problems with the banks. Big problems. They were like merciless dragons, ready to pounce on people. Foreclosures were always imminent, a constant worry. Growing up at that time I thought that the word *bank* was a swear word because of the tone with which it was used. They were looked upon with fear and distrust, to be avoided, if at all possible. People loaned each other small amounts. Promissory notes and interest were unknown. Collateral was never needed. Debts were repaid promptly and without fail.

Going into town for provisions meant doing favors for the neighbors as well: buying some necessities, picking up mail, taking some small items to market, or delivering messages. Whoever could spare a day would make the trip, leaving the others free to continue with their work. There was no need for each family to make the twenty-five-mile trek to town separately, for its own small needs.

So when the time came to start building the house, there had already been much discussion and speculation among the neighbors. Men came to the site and, with serious countenances, pointed and gesticulated, nodded or shook their heads. It had to stand lengthwise, so that the door to the north would be on the side overlooking the yard. Another door and windows must face the south, for the sun, and also windows on the east and west sides. They measured how many steps in length the house would be, and how many in width. Then they talked and deliberated, and measured again with a stick. Not surprisingly, when the construction finally began, all sorts of tools were at hand. Everybody had brought something, and the tools were assembled together and put to use.

Then, one day, Mother said we were going to see the new house. It was a walk of just over half a mile, diagonally across the homestead. I was five years old, and Ivas was two. Mother carried him in her arms. Her face was flushed with excitement. She walked briskly, and impatiently prodded me to hurry. I was excited, too, as I skipped along trying to keep up with her. We wended our way through the forest, bushes, sloughs, and tall grass to a clearing on top of a hillock. And there it was: a house! A real house!

I can only surmise what my mother's feelings were. Being an emotional person and having endured the hardship of primitive housekeeping in the hut, her excitement, and expectations, must have been boundless. No longer would she need to bear the ordeal of the mud hut, with its mud roof, mud floor, and mud walls.

As we stood in front of the new house, it looked so big and tall. The pale clean logs made it seem magnificent. Mother and I stared in awe. We were actually going to live in it! Well, not just yet, for it was still only a shell. Windows and doors had to be installed; the floors had to be laid; and, of course, it needed to be plastered. Plastering was a major operation. It was a task mainly for the women, who had the expertise, but men helped and were responsible for providing the materials. The men dug a pit in the yard and dumped in a wheelbarrow full of clay and some fine straw. Clay was not easy to come by, for most of the soil in the area was black or sandy loam. It was necessary to travel farther away to find the special clay patches. Water was heated in a big cast-iron boiler, which was used mainly for heating water for the animals in winter. The hot water was poured over the clay and straw, and the women went to work.

They tucked the hems of their skirts around their waists and, in their bare feet, trampled the mass until it became smooth and sticky. Two or three women pranced around at a time. They knew when the clay was just the right consistency. The men then carried it in buckets to the house, where other women and girls were ready to proceed with the next step. Each woman would pick up a big handful, shape it into proper form, and, with full force, throw it into the space between the logs, so that it penetrated through to the other side. They worked hard and diligently as a team. Starting at the ceiling, on scaffolds, they gradually moved down to the floor, completing each wall, log by log, before going to the next. When the whole house was plastered, it was left to dry. Then a final smooth layer of clay was applied by hand. Once that dried, the walls were ready for whitewash. The floor and ceiling were made of wood. The ceiling was quite fancy. It was constructed of narrow tongue-and-groove boards, bought at the lumber store. The floor was made of wide, homemade boards. It was all so clean, and new, and wonderful.

Finally, the house was completed and we moved in. Ivas was three years old and I was six. It was early fall. The weather was cold, windy, and raw. There was still no snow on the ground, only a coating of white frost. The two big rooms on the second floor were not yet finished, so we all occupied the two big rooms on the ground floor. All four rooms were the same size. Mother and Father had a new, big bed in the second room, which was originally meant to be a sitting room, and later became one. Ivas and I slept on another big bed in a corner of the kitchen. There was also a settee in another corner of the kitchen, and sometimes I slept on that.

But in the cold winter weather, our parents said we would be warmer together on the big bed. A wood-burning kitchen stove and a wood-burning space heater in the second room heated the house. At night, the house became extremely cold. Our parents would get up several times during the night to refuel the stoves, but wood burns fast and the house remained at a sub-zero temperature. Because we slept under feather *pyrynas* (duvets), we were more or less comfortable. In the morning, there would be hoarfrost on the pillows and covers around our faces.

Mother was impatient to make improvements to the house, because it was still in an unfinished state when we first moved in. By 1921, my parents could spare a little bit of money for improvements. Father sold a few sacks of grain and a couple of hogs to get the money. Mother gave this project her full attention, and tackled it with vim and resolution. No one dared offer any help or advice.

"It will be the way I want it," she said.

The walls were given a finishing coat of fine clay plaster, and then painted with white kalsomine, a type of whitewash. The wood floors were scrubbed clean and painted light brown in one room, but left natural in the kitchen and in the two rooms upstairs. All other woodwork, the doors, door and window frames, and the stairs to the second floor were left natural.

Then came the interesting part: arranging the furnishings. The big bed was placed in the corner of the second room, on the first floor. A crude old table with wobbly legs was set under a window. It had a drawer in it where Father kept receipts and other important papers. A new trunk, with fancy ornamentation, for storing linens (all made from flour sacks) and undergarments, was placed in the corner opposite the bed. A long bench, which Father had made, was placed under a window, along the south wall. In the third corner, a wood-burning heater was set up, with a wood box beside it. In the fourth corner, along the inside wall, was a plank, with hooks for hanging clothes, with a Singer sewing machine beside it.

A massive wood-burning stove was in the kitchen. Attached to it was a small boiler, with about a ten-gallon capacity, for heating water. Every day it was filled with water from the well; that was mainly my responsibility. Adjacent to the stove was a sturdy, hardwood buffet, which Father had bought at an auction. It held our limited supply of dishes, some cooking utensils, and a drawer full of towels. These were made from flour sacks that had been ripped open, washed, and bleached sparkling white. Between the stove and the buffet sat a big wood-box piled high with firewood. The table, at which all meals were served, stood against the west wall under the window. Between the stairs and the outside door was the washstand and basin, with a towel hanging above, and next to it, the water pail with a dipper on a stool.

Upstairs were two beds, and no other furniture. The ample space was useful for storage. All staple foods, flour, rice, buckwheat, and other cereals, were kept there. And in another corner were out-of-season boots and clothing, and a few tools, for use around the house when the workshop was inaccessible during winter storms. I particularly remember the bulky bearskin coat hanging there. My father wore it on his numerous trips north into the bush for logs. For some reason, that old coat assumed a special significance for me. I brought it with me to Toronto, where it hung in my basement, a sentimental piece of memorabilia, until I sold the house and finally discarded it.

Over the windows, Mother hung fine gauze curtains and dark green blinds. The blinds were to screen out the hot summer sun, rather than for privacy. Privacy was assured, since the farmyard was isolated. Colorful wall calendars, gifts from the banker and the storekeepers, were tacked on the wall, along with a few flower-seed packages with pretty pictures of flowers on them. A couple of attractive arrangements of red crepe-paper roses, which Mother and I had made, were fastened in special places. Mother would carefully consider just where the exact suitable spot would be. I held them against the wall, while she stepped back to scrutinize the effect. The calendar over the basin, in the kitchen, had a pocket for holding small items: a comb, scissors, a pencil, clothespins, and hairpins. In it was also a skeleton house key, which was never used. No one ever thought of locking anything up. Not in the entire fifty years that my parents lived in their home was it ever considered necessary. There were no thefts.

I remember, in school, listening with amazement to the teacher, who repeatedly told us that it was wrong to steal. We were baffled by his apparent anxiety. It was a well-known fact to everybody that nobody stole. We had never heard of any such deeds being committed except in stories. Even many years later, when I lived in Toronto, I still left my house unlocked while I was absent, for hours, sometimes for an entire day.

The climax of my mother's decorating, after all those lesser objects and articles were in place, was the hanging of the two icons. They had been bought, in the early years, while we still lived in the hut. Mother had diligently saved one egg every day or so, from the few that our four hens laid. She also managed to save a few pounds of butter, from our single cow. Father drove by wagon team to Lamont to sell them and used the money to buy the icons. One icon depicted Jesus Christ, with a bleeding heart, and the other was of Mary, Mother of God. Father had framed them under glass, with wooden frames that he had made himself and painted black. In the hut, they had hung on each side of the small window; and now, in the new house, they were also carefully displayed on each side of the window. But this larger window was surrounded by a broad wall space that was devoted, solely, to showing them off to particular advantage, as only such most holy images deserved.

In the evenings, we knelt before them to pray; and whenever we passed by them, we crossed ourselves. I usually did it very quickly. The icons were observed with solemn devoutness and awe. Later, when my brother George went to war, Mother was sometimes caught, standing before them, whispering prayers and crossing herself. For us children, their presence in the house was a constant reminder that all our actions were watched and monitored, both the good and the bad. Our chances of going to heaven after death depended on those icons. Occasionally, I would summon some courage and look at the faces. Sometimes they seemed benevolent, but at other times mysterious and unrelenting. It was impossible to ignore their existence, no matter how one tried.

Years later, the house underwent another refurbishing. A front sunroom was constructed and a back sunroom was built off the kitchen. A new stove, with a cream-colored enamel front, was acquired, as well as a dining table and chairs. We bought a chesterfield, put linoleum on the kitchen floor, installed a wardrobe cupboard, and displayed assorted knickknacks. A special luxury item, for which Mother had yearned and for which she had patiently waited and saved, was added to our home's décor: a chiming mantle clock. Mother greeted the cardboard box, when it arrived from the store, with unbounded joy and pleasure. We children had to stand back and wait before we were allowed to feast our prying eyes on this magical wonder. It sat in its place of honor. And henceforth, it was treated with a distinct reverence, Mother's most prized possession.

Andriy's Break

DANNY EVANISHEN

Danny Evanishen was inspired to write "Andriy's Break" because, he says, "It is a story that needs telling. Most Canadians are unaware of the internment of Ukrainians in World War I. Even those who do know about it shrug it off. These were real people, innocent people."

Ivan Hryhoryshchuk, killed while trying to escape Spirit Lake Internment Camp in Quebec, 7 June 1915

The original story was written by Danny's father in Ukrainian and published in the newspaper Ukrainian Voice *in 1988. Danny expanded it after doing research on the Ukrainian internment of World War I.*

Many internees were shot trying to escape. For example, John Kondro, aged seventeen, escaped from a British Columbia camp on April 10, 1916. He was never found. Andrew Grapko, aged eighteen, was killed while attempting to escape from the camp in Brandon, Manitoba.

There are instances of tamed moose on the prairies.

"*M*y son Andriy is not all that clever, but he is not crazy, either," said Joe Kozlowski on his farm near Brandon, Manitoba. Joe and his wife Maria had come to Canada in 1901 with their son Andriy. Their son Petro was born in Canada three years later.

In 1915, Andriy was seventeen years old. He was a sturdy lad, with dark blond hair and blue eyes, a typical Ukrainian farm boy. Because he was something of a dreamer, he was not understood by many people. But his mother understood him and it was she who soothed his fears and dried his tears when he was a baby. Andriy loved his mother, and would do anything to make her happy.

Andriy may have been a dreamer, but most of his dreams were realistic. He dreamed of being as good a farmer as his father, and he was well on his way to achieving his goal. Andriy's family had been farmers for many generations in the Old Country, and Andriy was destined to follow in his father's footsteps. He willingly did all that was asked of him, and he learned well.

Andriy's favorite season was the spring. Things started to grow in the spring, and he could work outside much more comfortably. All winter long, he would gaze dreamily through the frosted window and say, "Maybe today the weather will break, and we will have spring again." He said it so often that his family and friends began to refer to any break in the weather or rise in temperature as "Andriy's Break." It made Andriy feel good to hear it.

Andriy loved taking care of the little family's horses, their pride and joy. After working in the fields, he took the horses back to the barn, where he brushed them down and made sure that they were properly fed and watered. He always talked to the horses, and they seemed to understand him. They may not have understood the words, but their calmness was due to Andriy's gentle kinship with the beasts of the earth.

One warm spring morning, shortly after Andriy's Break had really finally occurred, Andriy was out in the field, picking rocks, when he heard a strange sound in the bush. He knew it was a young animal, but he didn't know what kind. He walked carefully toward the noise and entered the bush, keeping a watchful eye on his surroundings. If this was a young bear, its mother might well be around.

Near a pond, surrounded by bush, Andriy found the source of the noise. He was surprised to see a young moose. It was standing next to the body of its dead mother. Andriy couldn't tell how the mother had died, but he thought it might have been a heart attack, as he could see no marks on her body.

The young moose was not afraid of Andriy. It was probable that the animal had never seen people before, and Andriy was certainly not a threatening figure. He was easily able to lead the ungainly creature home. It took some time, but the moose instinctively trusted Andriy. Once home, Andriy led the moose into the barn and then ran to the house to get some milk.

"Mama! Mama! Come and see what I have found," he cried.

Mama poured some milk and helped Andriy try to feed the hungry moose. It was a complete comedy; the moose had no idea of milk in pails. When Andriy pushed the moose's nose into the milk, it snorted and sprayed milk all over the barn. The moose finally got the idea and had a good feed.

As summer passed, Andriy was able to train the moose. He taught it to pull a small wagon he had made, and the two of them became quite a fixture in the countryside. Andriy and his Moose, they were called.

As the moose grew, he got stronger. Eventually he was able to pull a bigger cart. Andriy and his two best friends, Mykhailo and Vasyl, often went to country dances in the cart. They had to be sure to tie the moose some distance from the schoolhouse or barn, wherever the dance was, so that the moose would not be frightened by all the noise.

Most of the time Andriy had fun at the dances, although he did not dance. He was too shy to appear on the dance floor. He spent most of his time watching and enjoying the music.

Unfortunately, some English boys in the neighborhood were troublemakers. They seemed to enjoy bullying the other boys and trying to steal their girlfriends.

Andriy was confronted by the leader of the gang at one dance. He put his face belligerently in front of Andriy's face and sneered, "My name is William. What's your name, little boy?"

"My name is Andriy."

"Andriy? What the hell kind of name is that? Are you one of those bohunks we've been trying to keep away from our women?" was the reply. *Bohunk* was an insult; it was the word the English used for lower-class immigrants from Central and Eastern Europe.

Luckily, some of Andriy's friends heard the exchange, and

they gathered around Andriy. Like most bullies, the leader of the gang backed off when he saw that they were outnumbered. But for the rest of the evening, William and his gang whispered viciously amongst themselves, pointed at Andriy and his friends, and made threatening gestures.

As it turned out, though, nothing further happened. There were too many of Andriy's friends at the dance. The bullies got tired of making noise, and they wandered off to another dance, where they hoped to have more luck starting a fight.

After the dance, Andriy and his friends found the moose where they had left him, and they rode home, singing the songs they had heard at the dance.

Since he could not read when he first arrived in Canada, Joe Kozlowski often took his young family to the local reading society. Someone was there to read the newspaper and other material for the local people. It was at the reading society that they learned of events in the world. It was where they learned that Canada was at war with Austria.

"This is good," the people said. "Now, maybe, we can all chip in and help to throw those Austrians out of our homeland."

Several of the men and older boys immediately made plans to join the Canadian Army.

"They say they pay wages in the army," Mykhailo said.

"Really?" asked Vasyl. "God knows our farms cannot make enough to give us cash money!"

"Tato, do you think I should go?" asked Andriy.

"I don't know, Andriy," was the reply. "It is true that we could use the cash money, but I think your mother would worry about you."

Once the idea was in his head, however, nothing could dissuade Andriy. "We need the money," he said. "And I was told we would do much training in Canada, so the war might even be over before I would have to go to fight. Petro is old enough to help with the harvest, so you don't really need me as much, for the next while, anyway."

Finally, Joe and Maria reluctantly agreed that Andriy would go to town to see if he could enlist. Neighbors Mykhailo and Vasyl, who were a year or two older than Andriy, decided to go with him, and the three set off. They just happened to get to town on a day when the local policeman was in a bad mood, and, unfortunately, the policeman saw the boys just as they got to the train station.

"Come here, boys," said the policeman. "You are coming with me."

The policeman grabbed Andriy by his collar, and held onto Vasyl's arm while he led the bewildered boys to the police office.

"What have we done?" asked Andriy. "Where are you taking us?"

"You just keep quiet, boy, and you won't get hurt," was the reply.

The three boys were dragged off to the police office, where they were locked in a room with several other men from the neighborhood.

"What is happening to us?" asked Andriy.

"This English policeman thinks we Ukrainians are enemies of Canada," said one of the men. "Canada is at war with Austria, and because most of us came from the part of Ukraine under Austria's rule, they think we are Austrians, too. They think we're some kind of traitors. So they are sending us to a concentration camp."

"Even though we have done nothing," said John, who was one of Andriy's neighbors. "If they gave me a chance, I would join the Canadian Army and help to kick those Austrians out of our homeland. But they don't believe that, so they arrest us."

"But what about my moose?" cried Andriy. "What about my

poor mother? She will certainly worry about me. Won't they even let us go home to say good-bye?"

"Not a chance," said John. "And for this we came to help build this famous Canada?" Several of the men growled in sympathy with this last remark.

None of the men who had been rounded up was allowed to go home. If some of their luckier neighbors hadn't seen what was happening, all the Ukrainian men would have disappeared, and their families would never have known what had happened to them.

The next day the men were shipped to the camp. They were immediately put to work. Andriy, being a simple soul, was still confused by events, but he applied himself willingly and patiently. He never refused any job, even though others would not do what they thought of as dirty work. Because Andriy was known to be good with animals, he was soon helping to take care of the camp's horses. The horses were used as mounts for the guards and also to haul logs out of the bush and around the camp.

None of the internees liked cleaning barns. They often teased Andriy because he would do such work with a light heart. The teasing was mostly good-natured, for the internees realized that if Andriy did not do this work, they would have to do it themselves.

"You are good at that work, Andriy," they said to him. "The horses are like your brothers." Andriy would smile his shy smile and carry on with his work. He never took offense at any of the teasing.

Conditions at the camp were fairly primitive, as it had not been in existence for long. The internees were made to build their own barracks and cookhouse and dig their own latrines. While they built a permanent camp, they slept in drafty tents that leaked when it rained. Luckily, they were able to get most of the buildings finished before winter. Then they were sent out to work. They logged and built roads and bridges, even though they were not properly dressed. It was a rough existence.

Andriy was lucky, as much of his work was in the barn. When the horses went to work in the bush, however, he went with them. The men had to cut logs for their buildings and for the sawmill. It was hard work. And it got much harder when the snow fell, and they struggled to keep warm.

The food was not very good, either. The men were given barely enough to survive and they were constantly hungry. "Some Englishman has the contract to supply food for this camp," one man said. "I heard about this before. The contractor gets lots of money for good food, but he gives us the junk that he can't sell anywhere else. The guards get good food, so they don't even know what is happening. They wouldn't care, even if they did know."

The guards' lives were not much better than those of the internees. They also lived in log huts and had to struggle to keep warm, but their lot was easier because they had better clothing and food. Even so, lots of guards were replaced, for one reason or another. When a new contingent of guards arrived one day, Andriy was horrified to recognize his old nemesis, William the bully.

Andriy kept a low profile when William and his partner Eddie were on duty. He hoped that they would not recognize him. But one day William spotted Andriy.

"So it's you," said William. "This is what you get for trying to be better than us. We're not even supposed to talk to you, but I thought I would warn you not to turn your back on us." William strode off, laughing his mean laugh.

As the weather got colder and the men's boots and clothing wore out, survival became harder. But Andriy's willingness to take care of the horses meant that he spent a lot of time in the barn. For this small benefit Andriy was grateful, even though the other internees still occasionally teased him.

In the evening, in the barracks, the men discussed their situation. "We have done nothing wrong," they said. "Why have we been put in prison?" At these times, Andriy listened to the men, but did not often take part in the discussions. He was just as bewildered as they were.

"We must be careful," said Vasyl. "These guards are mostly old men and young boys, and they have been told that we are dangerous, so they are afraid of us. That makes them even more dangerous. Lots of them have guns, and I don't think they know how to use them. So make sure you don't do anything that would scare them, as they might just shoot," he added anxiously, aiming a pretend rifle at his mates.

Christmas was coming, and this posed a problem for Andriy. Christmas was the most important holiday for his family; they had always been together for Sviat Vechir, or Holy Night. It was a time of quiet and love. No quarreling was allowed to mar the peace of the season.

Andriy naïvely asked the camp commander for permission to go home for the holiday. But the authorities were in no hurry to make any such decisions. The boy waited and waited. Finally he asked again if he could go home.

"If you bother us once more with this silly request, you may never go home ever again! Now go back to work, like a good boy," he was told gruffly.

Time was going by. Andriy was afraid to ask again, so he decided he would go home for a few days, without permission, so that his mother would not worry about him. He had not heard from his parents, and he was sure they would be worried. After the holiday, he would come right back.

The next afternoon, Andriy was working in the barn. He thought, at first, that he could simply walk out the door and go away from the camp. But he realized they might see him and make him come back. Perhaps when they were having their supper—but there was always someone on guard. The window at the back of the barn... they might not see him... he tried one window and found that it was too small for him.

Looking up, he saw the door of the hayloft. He climbed up to the door, opened it slightly, looked around to make sure nobody was outside, and squeezed his way out. He jumped down onto the snow on the manure pile behind the barn and rolled to a stop. He had bumped his arm, but was otherwise unhurt. He walked toward the barbed-wire fence, intending to crawl under.

The guards at the camp were all at supper, except for William and Eddie. They usually had to stand guard until their superiors had had their meal. The two of them were on patrol. They heard Andriy drop from the barn. They peeked around the corner and saw that Andriy was almost at the fence.

"He's making a break!" Eddie exclaimed. "What should we do?"

"Our orders are to shoot anyone trying to escape," said William excitedly.

"But is he trying to escape? Look, he is almost at the fence!"

"We have to shoot," said William. "If we try to stop him, he might hurt us. And orders are orders."

"Then you do it," said Eddie.

Just as he neared the fence, Andriy heard someone yell, "Halt!" Before he could turn to explain, the shot was fired. He pitched forward, face first, in the soft snow. He tried to rise, but was only able to say, "Mama!" before he fell again.

At the shot, all the guards and some of the internees came running to see what was happening. There was a great uproar when they saw Andriy. He was lying in the snow, in a pool of his own blood. The guards immediately made a ring around their mates with their guns ready.

"Steady, men!" yelled the captain. "You prisoners go back to your barracks immediately. We will take care of this!"

The outraged internees were driven back to their barracks,

where they were left to try to make sense out of what had happened.

The two guards were commended by their captain. "You have followed orders well," he told them. "And don't worry about shooting this guy. He's only a bohunk."

Andriy's lifeless body was dragged back to the barracks. He was buried without ceremony in the camp's new cemetery. The internees were not told about the burial. The guards who dug the grave were the only witnesses. Andriy's parents were eventually sent a letter informing them of his death. The official record said "killed while attempting to escape."

Andriy's brother Petro did not have much success with the young moose. It eventually wandered off into the forest. It is a matter of record that, in the winter, a moose used to bed down in the camp cemetery. It even knocked over some of the crosses on the graves. Some people say it was Andriy's moose. He had come to Andriy's grave to be with his old friend again.

Tribute to My Grandmother

KIM PAWLIW, *thirteen years old*

Canadian
But of Ukrainian origin
Your freedom was taken away
Your belongings were confiscated that day

They took you and your family
Moved all of you to Abitibi
They brought you so far
To an Internment camp at a time of war
It was misery
You worked there for no money

We must remember this story
To keep it in memory
For it is all true
Dear Baba, I will never forget you

During World War I, Kim's grandmother, Stéphania Mielniczuk, was just a child, yet she and her family were imprisoned at Spirit Lake Internment Camp as enemy aliens. Here is Kim's original tribute, written in French:

Hommage à Ma Grand-Mère

Canadienne,
D'origine ukrainienne,
Ta liberté t'a été enlevée,
Tes biens confisqués.
Ils t'ont pris ta maison
Et emmenée dans un camp de concentration.
C'était la guerre
Et la misère
Vous avez travaillé et peiné
Sans être payé.
Il faut se rappeler le passé
Pour ne jamais recommencer.
Repose en paix, chère Baba,
Moi je ne t'oublie pas.

Kim's grandmother, Stéphania Mielniczuk Pawliw, as a child with her parents. Taken February 14, 1920, a couple of years after they were released from the internment camp at Spirit Lake, Quebec

1919

It's Me, Tatia

Brenda Hasiuk

One day, I saw a very old woman, like any other old woman, sitting in an olive-green armchair, looking out the window.

Outside the window was a specific neighborhood, namely the north end of Winnipeg, but the chair could have been any other chair in any other nursing home. It seems her story is an ordinary one—not unlike the story of my grandmothers and my great-grandmothers and thousands of others—but still she sits there, a mystery.

What is she thinking? I know this much. I know her century was one of cultural clashes and social upheaval and great, great labors. I know she lived in a place where immigrant settlers broke their backs for better futures while displacing generations of Aboriginal people in the bargain, and where an exploited working class staged a general strike that would fail miserably while still advancing the notion of rights and standards that define our workplaces today. I know her mind and body are finally exhausted.

But what does she think of in those moments when what's passed is all that's left?

Never got found, never got found, never got found.

I hear some glass break down on the street, and then you stick your head in the door and call my name.

"Tilly? You all right? Why are you up? You have trouble breathing?"

I must've made a noise. Cried out. God knows why, because it's the same every night—the beer bottles, or the sirens, or the snowplow waking me up in the middle of God knows when. It's always the same now; I'm woken up by the slightest little thing. I'm like a cat, always dozing, always waking up.

This time, though, I'm all the way up, in the olive-green chair by the window.

"Why are you not in bed?"

Go away, it's not your business, I want to say, but I hold my tongue. How did I get into the green chair?

Mrs. Maria Litwicki, original settler of Ethelbert, Manitoba, arrived in Canada as a young woman, died at age ninety-three

"You gave us a scare before," you say, still in the doorway. "It's cold out there; the wind chill will freeze your skin in two minutes. What were you thinking, going outside? Huh?"

I remember now. I could feel your hands, your little brown hands, no bigger than a child's, shaking as you led me back, gripping hard with those little hands.

Back in the room, you had put on the television and filled a foot basin with hot water.

31

"See? It's your favorite," you said. "Cops and robbers. That one there, in the toque, he looks like bad news."

You fidgeted with your little necklace, the way you always do when you don't know what to do next. But this time, it reminded me of something. *Never got found,* my mind said. *Never got found, never got found.*

I'd seen something, out there in the cold. But what was it? Someone had been crying maybe, but who?

Now, in the middle of the night, all I know is that you won't leave until I say something; let you know I haven't died on your watch.

"I'm fine. This housecoat is warm. I'm fine here."

You don't go away; just stand their fidgeting, moving the silly little cross back and forth along the chain. *You think you know what cold is,* I want to say. *You, who come from some island where there are probably palm trees and bananas.*

On the day I was born—sixty, seventy, maybe eighty years before you—the sod walls were completely iced in. Five, ten, twenty feet of snow, and the midwife couldn't come, and there wasn't enough kindling. And I was so small and feeble, like a runt pup; and so Mamo, Papo, and Johnny all got close on the bed and tried to keep me warm without suffocating me right there.

"Oi, you were shriveled like a prune, as if from the cold," Mamo said, "but the Virgin looked down on us."

When you sigh, still fidgeting and not going away, I want to throw something. How long has it been since I've wanted to throw something? *You think this is hard work,* I want to ask, *following the old people around?*

I've scrubbed toilets for a family with seven children, five nearly fully grown and still living in their parents' house. I've stood sorting eggs—who can count how many—until the cold seeped into my joints and I never moved the same again. But you have not known work until you've farmed the prairie, from nothing, with nothing but your bare hands.

All my childhood, I stooped over. What do you know about such things?

You shrug, like maybe you've heard what I'm thinking. "You need something, you let me know then."

As soon as you're gone, the anger dies away, just like that. I hated the work, hated all of it—in the fields, in the houses, in the factories. Who am I to begrudge you, who cuts my toenails with such care?

I reach into my pocket for a peppermint and wait for the words to come back. At first, I hear only a truck crunching over the snow-packed street, and my own sucking noise. It's so cold that the window is cloudy with truck exhaust.

Never got found, never got found, never got found.

This time, I'm back on the farm—clearing the roots and the rocks, cleaning the ashes from the oven, spreading hay over the shit.

I'm standing. My underwear and hairbrush, and some sauerkraut buns, are wrapped in a kerchief. I'm not thinking about being on the noisy train for the first time. I'm not thinking about the big city. I'm not thinking about missing this place, where the natives laugh at you while you stoop; laugh as they go by on their brown-and-white-spotted horses—with their funny boots and blankets, and babies tied to their backs.

I'm thinking about what I've heard—that some hired girls in the city have their own room, with a bed, a cupboard, and even a lamp.

Papo is outside, stooping over to dig, or pull, or skin something. Mamo is acting funny, walking back and forth across the new wooden floor like she still doesn't trust it yet and needs to keep trying it out. It's hot and sticky outside, not even a breeze, and the room is filled with steam and the bubble of boiling tomatoes.

"You work hard," Mamo says. "You work hard, Tatia. You work hard, and I'm sure Christ will reward you."

I can smell the buns in my bundle and want to eat one now, but they're for later. "Yes, Mamo."

Then Mamo stops and grabs a jar of stewed tomatoes from the table. "You take this, for later."

I take the jar and hold it out in front of me. Mamo is acting funny, and I don't know what to do with the tomatoes, so I put them back. "It might break."

Mamo turns away and gets her Bible. It's in the corner by the icons—where it always is. She holds it in her hands. "Fine," she says. Then she puts the Bible back and starts stirring over the pots, like she's been doing all day. "You do as you like. You're old now."

"The jar," I say. "It could break on the train."

But she doesn't turn around—and I'm already walking. Johnny and Lasia and Terry and Tanya have already stopped waving when she comes from behind, wiping her sweaty face with her apron. "You take this."

It's the tiny crucifix that she wears around her neck, the one all her babies pull at and get slapped over. She's looking at the ground. The sweat is dripping off her chin and I think she might be crying. But Mamo never cries.

"Be good, Tatia," sweaty Mamo says, "Christ be with you."

I walk away to the station, until my heels feel like they're being stuck with pins, until I am as sweaty as Mamo—until there's nothing left but road and the words sounding in my head.

Never got found, never got found, never got found.

Now, in the middle of the night, I watch the snowplow charge back and forth like an angry bull as it clears the street. Earlier, those words came to me once again.

It was before bedtime, right after I went outside. I remember someone had been crying, but that's all.

I heard them—*never got found, never got found, never got found*—as you stuck my feet in the basin, all business. "He was crying," I told you.

But you just turned up the television. "You just worry about yourself," you said. "If you get up on your own, you could fall down. Your grandchildren come here to see how you're doing. What would we tell them if something happened to you?"

I've marched these streets, I wanted to say. *I knew them before the stores closed and the hoodlums took over; before one granddaughter starting calling them "the core area," frowning like she knows something.*

I know them better than anyone—even now, when I look out the window and the streets are familiar—but so different that I look away. It's like when the young ones come, the great-grandchildren; they look familiar, but I can't get at their names. They all blur together like the bottom rows of an eye chart.

I don't care, I wanted to say. *Those grandchildren know no more than you do.*

Now, you with your fidgety little hands, you wouldn't believe the words that are coming to me—coming from so far away, and yet closer than ever. All my life, words have come to me like this. As a child, it was *never got found*, but there would be others. Like a nagging song that stays in your head, the words would repeat over and over and over again in my mind, steady and relentless.

It seems I only have to sit in this olive-green chair, in the middle of the night, and listen.

140 Montrose, 140 Montrose, 140 Montrose.
I'm carefully ironing Mrs. Sullivan's tea towels, white with little mauve flowers; folding first in halves, then in quarters. I'm shaking the feather pillows into pale yellow cases, careful not to catch the silk with my rough skin. I'm walking to Mass in my new muskrat coat, flushed hot from the long trolley ride across town.

After Montrose Street, everything here, on these streets, seems ugly and worn—the people, the sidewalks, the houses. It smells. And I'm starting to smell, too, just being here in the muskrat. Since when is it so warm in February?

140 Montrose, 140 Montrose, 140 Montrose.

I step around the melting piles of dog shit, there's no escaping the shit, going as fast as I can, sure to be late. And then, *smack*, there's nothing but pain behind my ear.

A voice shouts from behind and I turn. How long has it been since I've heard my language?

"You, what's your name?" A man is stepping right in the puddles, splashing his pant legs as he goes. "You—your name?"

"Tatia," I start to say, but then remember. "Tilly."

When he stops, he is close enough to touch, and he's breathing hard. He's only wearing a light shirt, open at the neck. "Well, Tatia-Tilly, let me tell you, you look like a bourgeois in that thing. That's why they threw the snowball." He clears his throat, spits into the slush. "Still, they shouldn't have thrown it, eh?"

He's speaking my language, but I don't really understand.

"Tell me, Tatia. Do you live around here?"

Even though I'm hot, I turn up the collar of my coat. I speak in English.

"I live with the Sullivans at 140 Montrose Street."

"Ah," he says. "A domestic. They couldn't pronounce Tatia?"

I don't know what to say. How would he know such a thing?

"You must be on your way to church, Tatia," he says, like he can read my mind. "That church—it's always the same. Stand up, sit down, sit down, stand up. Eh?"

I feel I should be angry, but there is something about him, stamping his wet feet to keep warm, that makes me smile. He is like no man I have ever seen—nothing like Papo; nothing like Mr. Sullivan.

"We're having a meeting over there in the park," he says.

He puts his hand under my elbow, clutches at the fur, and I

don't stop him. I know I am going to hell, and yet I let him lead me away.

"I'm Saul," he says. "Come."

Saul Solemen. Saul Solemen. Saul Solemen.

I'm polishing Mr. Sullivan's shoes as fast as I can, the sweet smelling polish flying *swish-swash, swish-swash,* over the leather. I'm washing the floor in what they call the "foyer," ring and swoosh, ring and swoosh—quick over white tile, then black, white tile, then black. I'm rocking to and fro on the trolley. The red book, hugged to my chest, so everyone can see—all the way to the deli, where Saul is looking at me with his hands in his chin—thin hands covered with fine, curly black hair. When he talks, the cigarette bounces on his lip.

"I thought it was so cold that you might not come. But I forgot; you have your bourgeois coat, Tatia. Warm February, cold March. What a place, eh?"

He keeps looking, his head in his hands, and I nod. I feel my face flushing and think of my sweaty mama standing over boiling tomatoes.

He takes the cigarette from his lips and points at me. "But you, Tatia, you don't look like a bourgeois. You have an open and honest face."

No one has ever said such a thing about my face before. *What do you do when you can't stop smiling?* I put my hand over my mouth.

"And a nice mouth," he says. Then he grabs the book and opens it to the marker. "Ah, our hero is in trouble."

I want to grab the book back. It's so good when he explains it—about bringing the power back to the working people so that no one will ever be owned again, not by man and not by religion. It's like the sound of his voice, sure and even, makes me forget that my calluses are bleeding, and no money has been sent home for months.

But the reading was hard and I haven't gotten very far.

"Any questions, Tatia?" he asks.

I think hard for one; I want to make sure he knows how hard I've tried.

"Salt of the earth," I say. "The book says 'salt of the earth,' and it sounds silly to say the earth is made of salt. What do they mean?"

He takes my hands, so big and chapped, and brushes my knuckles once, twice, three times with his thumb.

"It means *you*," he says. He stumps out his cigarette until it's no bigger than a pencil eraser. "You deserve a real worker's position, not cleaning up after some overpaid bureaucrat. I'll talk to some people. Don't worry."

I don't really understand, but I don't care. He goes to light another cigarette, and I can still feel his hands, thin hands covered with fine, curly black hair.

Salt of the earth. Salt of the earth. Salt of the earth.

I'm cutting brown packing paper at the plant. Swipe goes the knife, salt of the earth goes my head, swipe goes the knife, salt of the earth goes my head.

I'm walking home with Saul and Tereza from the strike meeting after work, and she is making fun of Mr. Rudy.

"C-c-c-come on, girls," she says. "You, you, you j-j-just went t-t-to the, the bathroom."

Even though it's night, it's warm enough to go without a jacket. And Saul keeps grabbing my shoulders, like he wants to dance right there, in the street.

Then Tereza is turning for home, and Saul's hand is under my elbow and we're in the alley behind the bakery. My back is against the brick wall, and he is so close I can hear the whistle from his nostrils.

"How long, Tatia?" he asks. "How long have we known each other, eh?"

I try to see his face, but it's too dark, and he is only a warm, whistling shadow.

"I think four months maybe," he says. "And now we're friends, no?"

All I want is to put my fingers in his curls. Would they feel soft and springy or thick and wiry? I reach up, and then I can feel his soft curls in my hand and taste the sour tobacco on his tongue, and somewhere, far away, there is the sound of the street.

He suddenly steps away and grabs my shoulders, like when we were walking.

"This," he says. "This, Tatia, is what it's all for. You see? Me, a Jew, and you, a peasant, and all the horrific past of greed and hatred—it will be history. It will be nothing but justice."

I touch his hair again, and then he is so close I can feel the buttons of his shirt, and the heat of his hands, and his legs, and his breath, so warm compared to the cool, hard bricks.

Me a Jew. Me a Jew. Me a Jew.

Swipe goes the knife, *me a Jew* goes my head, swipe goes the knife, *me a Jew* goes my head.

I'm standing in the toilet stall, holding up my skirt.

"T-t-t-times up," Mr. Rudy shouts.

I don't say anything, just stand there, holding my skirt, remembering my Papo.

"The Romanians are bastards, and the Jews are bootlickers," Papo said. "They're smart, the Jews; they know who butters their bread, and they only screw you 'cause you're a stinkin' Ukrainian, my friend," while Mamo mumbled prayers under her breath.

I run my hands over my stomach and my chest, like Saul did. I think of the spit flying from Papo's mouth, and then the tickling of Saul's tongue. I punch the wooden door of the stall with all my might. The latch breaks and hangs there, like it's dead.

I think of my Mamo and Papo, with no letter for months. I think of leaving the Sullivans before the sun is even up. Mamo's precious gift is still under the pillow. I think of Saul, who is a Jew, and who put his tongue in my mouth.

When Mr. Rudy calls again, I say I'm having female troubles and walk out the door.

Someone touches my shoulder and I jump.

When I open my eyes, it's too bright and I have to close them again. How did I get into the olive-green chair?

I can tell from your strange fishy smell that it's you.

"You want your breakfast here, or downstairs?"

You know I have no appetite, but still you bring it: the runny eggs and dry brown toast, the weak tea and apple juice. You put the tray down, on the round table beside me, and wait.

I turn away, and you cross your arms like you always do when I don't want your food.

"How are you going to feel better if you don't eat? Huh? You going to live on peppermints? Is that how you got to be so old? Living on the peppermints?"

You're smiling now, but I don't care. What was it that upset you last night? Someone was crying. I told you someone was crying. A little boy was crying outside.

I take the tea from the tray, but my hands aren't just stiff, like usual. They're shaky, like yours were last night. You have to mop up my housecoat with a paper napkin.

"You want the TV? There are some repeats on the cable. You like them."

You turn the chair so I can see, and more tea spills. But I don't say anything. On the screen, a judge is talking to a young man who looks guilty. The lawyer, a young woman, is walking back and forth in a short skirt.

I know these are my shows—the ones where they tell a whole story in one hour. The courtroom drama queen, one of the young ones calls me. But now the bright screen hurts my eyes, and the teacup is unsteady in my hands.

I wasn't done when you came in. What was I doing? What did I do before I was the courtroom drama queen? There was a time, I know, before the babies came and the endless eggs and the babies' babies, when there were no words in my head at all—when there was nothing to do but sit.

I close my eyes and try hard to remember. The words from the television blend like the great-grandchildren—familiar and forgettable.

I'm standing in the park, in the warm rain. Saul is at the front, somewhere I can't see him. There is nothing but a sea of shoulders, shiny and wet, so close around me I can hardly breathe.

"They shall not build, and another inhabit," a voice says from way up on the makeshift stage. "They shall not plant and another eat. For as the days of a tree are the days of my people, and mine elect shall long enjoy the work of their hands."

The words wash over me like the rain, clear and warm. Then there is nothing but a blast of fists in the air, and the shoulders begin to shout, almost altogether. It's nothing like the voices at mass, tired and sniffly. It's a giant wave of sound, all of us shouting together, terrible and wonderful. And when I touch my face I don't know if it's rain or tears.

"We're making history," Saul says after, gripping my shoulders like always. "They will talk of this, Tatia," he says, "and you can tell them that you were there." He grips harder, his black eyes shining like marbles. "You were there for the great Winnipeg strike of 1919."

For the first time, I'm doing nothing. I'm wasting time, placing a red seven on a black eight. I'm counting the cards—*one-two-three, one-two-three*—searching for the ones that I need, until there's no choice left but to shuffle the cards and start again, and again, and again. We have walked out on the Mr. Sullivans and the Mr. Rudys. We now sleep late, all of us, even the telephone operators and the policemen—all the workers and me.

I'm sitting out on the fire escape in my slip, waiting for the breeze, but all it brings is the smell of dirty diapers and other people's greasy supper. Why am I so tired? For ten hours I slept, and still didn't want to get out of bed. It's like my body weighs one thousand pounds.

I'm shuffling the cards, trying not to think of how many days it's been since Saul has come—how many days with no money, counting the cards, *one-two-three*, putting ace of hearts up top—when I hear the door.

I climb through the window, and he hands me a jar of crabapple jelly. His white shirt is stained dark around the collar, and his fingernails are black with ink.

The jelly makes me hungry. "There are no buns left," I say.

He takes the cigarette from his mouth and throws it across the floor. "No buns, Tatia? There are going to be arrests. That's what they're saying; there are going to be arrests."

I can't believe this—it's as if I'm still asleep and dreaming.

He makes a gurgling sound, puts his hands together like he's begging for spare change. "It's over, Tatia. The strike is dead. When the powerful are bastards and the weak are buffoons, what can you do?"

There are small bubbles of spit in the corners of his mouth. "Eh, Tatia, can you tell me? I bet you can't."

I can feel my blouse wet beneath the armpits. Who is this Saul, with black fingernails and bubbles of spit? I walk over to the smoldering cigarette and stomp it with my bare foot.

But he's looking somewhere else, somewhere out the window and far away.

Look at me! I want to scream. *Tell me that it doesn't have to be this way!*

What do you do, when you don't understand?

I kneel down and take his hands. I put them against my chest. "It's me… Tatia," I say.

He makes the gurgling sound again and then is on his knees.

"Tatia, you are so good," he says.

Suddenly the slip is at my waist. He picks me up, under the arms, and I lie back on the cot with the bruising springs. I close my eyes and feel him move, and there is pain. No worse, I think, than slamming your finger or spilling boiling water.

Then his tongue is tickling my neck, my cheek, my ear, while he whispers—and I'm not thinking of anything. There's only the pain, and his tongue, and the whispers—so good, so good—and it's all so close, and so awful, and so good that I can hardly stand it.

When he pushes hard, drops his chest down onto mine, I don't want it to stop.

Please, I want to say. *I don't want it to stop, so awful and so good, not for the Jews or for the Ukrainians, or for justice.*

He laughs at how I'm trembling. He covers me with a blanket, then his clothes, then mine. He puts all his weight on top of me, and still I tremble.

You take the teacup from my unsteady hand, but I don't want it to be a teacup.

I want it to be crabapple jelly. Saul took it from me, as he knelt, and let it roll across the floor.

"You're not talking to me today? You're not watching your shows?"

Not now, I want to say. *Please. This is too important.*

I want to know what happened to him.

I am Tilly, a hard-working stonemason's wife for over fifty years, but what about him? I was sleeping—and then Saul was gone.

My chest feels heavy, like he's still lying on top of me. I put a peppermint on my tongue, but it doesn't help. Every breath comes long and hard.

You, I want to say, standing there playing with the cross around your neck—you wouldn't understand. It's not good to be old and to never have believed enough.

I could never believe enough in the Virgin; never believe enough in justice.

My young ones have moved far away from here. They have foyers of their own. But no matter what, no matter how long I'm on this earth, I know these streets here still smell like the poor. I know you wear my Mamo's cross, but you still smell strange, and fishy, and I can't pronounce your name.

I know those shows on the television, with beginning, middle, and end; they're not real.

I know I will never know what happened to him. I didn't care to ask where he lived, as long as Saul came to me.

"You don't eat. You don't talk. You don't watch the TV. Are you going to at least have a bath? Huh? A nice bath?"

"A boy was crying," I say. "When I was outside last night. He was lost."

You walk away. Shout above the rush of water in the tub. "Why do you keep on about that? Don't you worry about that. They said his sisters came; they're looking for him. What was he doing out that late? That's what I want to know. Why do they let their kids wander out so late, all by themselves?"

I remember—it's the natives who live on these streets now. Last night it had been a native boy who was crying outside— maybe six years old, without a hat or mittens, his arms folded under his jacket like a chief. He was standing out of the wind, near the glass doors that slide open, just like that, crying.

"I don't know which way," he shouted. The snot was running into his mouth. "I don't know."

When I stepped outside, the air bit at my skin, and I almost fell down in surprise. How long had it been since the air bit through my sweater like that?

With his blue-black hair, the boy had almost disappeared into the dark. "What's your name?" I asked.

But he wasn't listening. "I don't know which way," he shouted.

Then your little brown hands were pulling me back inside the doors, away from the crying boy outside in the cold, back into the safe and stuffy room.

But you didn't know that the words were already there.

Never got found, never got found, never got found.

I'm walking in snow so deep that it's filling my boots. I can feel the cold metal of the shovel and the lantern through my mittens. And the cow and the oxen are somewhere behind, making low noises in the dark. I hate this—oh, how I hate it. But Mamo is coughing, and Johnny is coughing, and the others are too little to help.

Though I want to be done, I stop because the snow in my boots is melting against my legs. There are lots and lots of stars, but no fireflies. There are only fireflies in the summer, but why is that? Why can't they be there in the winter, too, when it's so dark—and you have to go out so early, and your legs sting so bad?

Never got found, never got found, never got found.

I'm walking again, through the deep snow, thinking of Papo's story.

"You remember this," he would say. "You remember the little one, little Mary, from nearby. It was spring planting, and—this is true because I worked the lines with her step-uncle, and he wasn't a liar—she left her work and went off to pick some wildflowers. At sundown, her family couldn't find her. Three days go by, and all they find is an Indian camp somewhere close, and then some people start seeing a bunch of them with a little white girl, but they never got found."

Then Papo would get the big jar from behind the flour sack, and pour some bootleg into a cup. He'd drink it in one big gulp and his face would turn bright red.

You could feel the heat, just standing next to him.

"You see," he'd say. "You work hard or the Indians, they'll snatch you away, and you'll go to live in the teepees."

I hang the lantern on a wooden post. Then I hold the shovel far out in front of me and bring it down with all my might.

Crack goes the ice, *never got found*, goes my head, *crack* goes the ice, *never got found*, goes my head, *slush* goes the ice, *never got found*, goes my head.

There is a small hole with black water inside. I step back, *one, two, three*, and then there is nothing but the sound of the animals, lapping and grunting.

They could still come, I think. *I'm alone, and the natives could come. They could come and steal me away to live in the forest— to wander with pots and babies on my back, to sit high on a horse and laugh.*

The animals are finished drinking, but I stay put. I am lost, lost, lost, but I'm not afraid.

I can't feel my legs, I say to myself in the dark.

But I must've said it out loud too because now you're standing over me, poking at me, upset again.

"You all right? You breathing all right? I can call an ambulance. We can go back to the hospital."

Leave me be! I want to shout. *Leave me be! Don't ruin it!*

I'm with the natives. They have swept me up, laughing, into the tall poplars. I'm with curly-haired Saul, who whispers, "So good" and makes me bleed until my bulky body falls away, and there's nothing but that feeling—so deep inside, painful and fine. I'm lost, lost, lost, where there is no Tatia, or Tilly, or stupid cows that need a drink.

But you poke and fidget, poke and fidget. You look at me

like my young ones do, trying to understand what I don't understand myself.

I didn't mean to upset you. "No," I say. "I'm fine. I want a bath."

You run to turn off the water, and then your small hands are on me. They're small, those hands, but when you help me up, I'm always surprised by their strength.

"You sure you're ready?"

Yes.

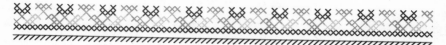

1932–1933

The Rings

Marsha Forchuk Skrypuch

This story is set during the 1932–33 Famine-Genocide. This genocide was orchestrated by Stalin in order to starve out the "kulaks"—Ukrainian farmers who refused to give up their land. In all, an estimated ten million people starved to death. In the midst of the Famine-Genocide, Stalin invited foreign journalists to tour the countryside so they could see for themselves that there was no famine. Many journalists were sympathetic to the communist cause, and they stayed on the official tour and took things at face value. Others saw the truth but reported lies in order to stay in favor with Stalin. Famous Famine-Genocide deniers include Walter Duranty

1932–33 Famine-Genocide in Soviet Ukraine—mass burial near Kharkiv

of the New York Times *and playwright George Bernard Shaw. There were a few honest journalists, like Malcolm Muggeridge and Gareth Jones, who heroically reported the truth and were scorned for it.*

There are accounts of people who escaped from soviet-occupied Ukraine and offered eyewitness testimony about the Famine-Genocide. Many were collected and published in 1953 in a book called Black Deeds of the Kremlin: A White Book, Volume 1: Testimonies, *edited by S.O. Pidhainy. Since the fall of the Soviet Union, more firsthand accounts have surfaced. A good online resource is:* www.faminegenocide.com *"The Rings" is based on a number of these firsthand accounts. After I wrote the story in 1999, I came across other accounts with eerie parallels to my own story; it made me realize how common the experience of Danylo in "The Rings" really was.*

Danylo's sharpest memory was of hunger.

When his father had refused to sign the papers handing over their tiny farm to the state, his family earned the label *pidkurkul*—or poor farmer who sympathizes with the kulaks.

His father knew that the communists would send in the Red Army to confiscate their grain, so he had mixed some wheat with the chaff and hidden it in the loft. He had also put the best wheat, for sowing, up in the rafters. Danylo's mother had hidden a sack of grain in the chimney.

The soldiers who came were a rough and brutal lot. They were not from the village, and they spoke Russian, not Ukrainian. They brought with them a stabber—a device made of a sharp-pronged stick with a bag on the end—to collect evidence of grain.

As one of the soldiers carried an armful of his father's hidden grain to the waiting cart, Danylo rushed forward and grabbed back some stalks of wheat. "Why are you doing this?" he cried.

The man said something in Russian that sounded like a curse. Another Red Army soldier opened the *pich* (oven) and confiscated the fresh loaves of bread baking there. They loaded all the food into the cart and took it away.

A few pieces of stale bread on the rubbish pile had somehow been missed. Danylo's family—his father, his mother, and three younger brothers—survived on these crusts and water for a couple of days. His baby sister Larissa was still at his mother's breast, one less mouth to feed.

Danylo watched as those around him appeared to shrink. His mother remarked one day, as she washed her face, that she could feel every bone in her skull. Later, when Danylo carried the soapy basin of water outside to empty it, he found her wedding ring, which had slipped off. She had not noticed. His mother had not been able to get the silver band past her knuckle for years. Danylo dried it on his shirt, and brought it back in to her. From then on, she wore it on a cord of leather around her neck.

When the crusts of bread were gone, one day passed with no food at all, just water. Danylo's feet and stomach began to swell with the first signs of starvation. His father caught and skinned a stray cat, which sustained them a few more days. But Danylo's four-year-old brother, Anatoly, swelled up and died. Danylo caught a hedgehog, and the remaining family survived on that for a while.

As winter set in, the rats, cats, dogs, and birds in the village disappeared. Danylo learned, like everyone else, that one must eat at least one morsel, each and every day, to keep oneself from swelling. If the swelling set in, your feet and belly would get so huge that you wouldn't be able to move. At that point, you could only sit and wait to die. When his mother began to starve, Danylo couldn't bear to look at her body, ballooning out grotesquely, as if it were about to burst. Her swelling caused what little milk she had been able to produce to stop. And so Larissa died. His mother died the next day, then ten-year-old Vasyl, and then seven-year-old Ivan.

Danylo and his father said prayers for the dead. His father reverently removed the cord that held her wedding ring from around his wife's neck. Before putting it around his own neck, he slipped off his own wedding ring and strung it on the cord.

In their small home, Danylo and his father sat with their dead loved ones for hours, perhaps days. What was time, anyway? It wasn't until the corpses began to stink that they dragged their family beyond the threshold. The village authorities had dug a huge pit in the graveyard. Each morning they sent a cart around to all the houses, collecting the bodies. They dumped the bodies into the pit until it was full. And then they dug a new one.

"Perhaps I was a fool not to sign our land away," Danylo's father wondered aloud one day. Then he and his son walked to the collective, intending to sign up. But even from the road, they could see that the workers in the state farm were no better off than the kulaks. The only people who were not starving were the Communist Party members, and they had confiscated the grain in the first place, so Danylo and his father returned home.

They resorted to boiling shoe leather and drinking it as broth, but this did not stave off the swelling. Word broke that a horse had starved to death in the commune, so Danylo, his father, and the few other surviving villagers walked to the collective, knives in hand, to carve up the horse. Without waiting to cook the meat, Danylo sat down on the ground and cut it into bloody chunks, devouring a morsel on the spot. The horse meat that they carried away lasted for several weeks.

When another horse died, on a state farm, Danylo and his father tried to repeat their success. But the Communist Party members foiled their plan. The horse was thrown into a pit and covered with acid. By the time Danylo and his father got there, most of the flesh had sizzled away. His father threw himself on the horse anyway. He cut off a hunk of still-intact flesh from the horse's hind quarter. Danylo tried to pull it away, but his father had already cut off some smaller bits and had swallowed some poisoned meat. His father doubled up with pain, almost immediately, and died that night.

Danylo said a prayer for his father. He sat beside the cold body from dusk until dawn. It wasn't until he heard the creaking wheels of the corpse wagon that Danylo broke his meditations. As he dragged his father's corpse over the threshold in the early morning light, a glint of silver shone from the leather cord around his father's neck. With the corpse collectors only yards away, Danylo reached down and undid the cord. As he retied it around his own, he noticed that the two silver wedding rings looked unnaturally large.

Danylo walked through the house one last time, as if to imprint the image on his memory. It was nothing more than a one-room mud shack. Everything of value had long been bartered for scraps of food. There was one small, sharp knife, so he took it. The only remaining item was a silver spoon that had been passed down, mother to daughter, for generations. It was his mother's prized possession. Danylo carefully wrapped it in a bit of cloth and placed it inside his shirt. He stepped outside and walked through the frozen strip of land that constituted their family farm. For the sake of this meager property, his whole family had been killed. How could he leave this place? His family had farmed this small patch of earth for uncounted generations. Danylo despaired at the thought of abandoning it. With his family gone, this was all he had in the world, yet he knew that staying guaranteed his death. If he could somehow survive, perhaps he could reclaim it one day.

As he walked down the main street and away from his home for the last time, he was struck by the absolute silence. No bird sang; no child ran in the street.

Danylo's uncle had a farm about ten kilometers away. Danylo and his siblings had been taken there once with his parents for a family wedding, and so he knew the general direction. He set off, hoping that things would be better there. He was so weak with hunger that his legs wobbled, but he had no choice but to forge ahead. He rested frequently, nibbling on bugs and early spring shoots of grass.

When he got to his uncle's home, he realized that things were just as bad there. Going through the motions of hospitality, his aunt offered him a stew made of boiled water and grass. Danylo ate it, with his hollow-eyed uncle, aunt, and their children looking on. He thanked them, but he knew that he must leave. Their generosity in the midst of such dire need touched his heart.

Twenty kilometers beyond his uncle's farm was a town with a train station, and so Danylo set out for there. Perhaps a train would be his salvation. The town was not much better off than Danylo's village, although not everyone was starving. The street was lined with swollen people. But there were also market stalls selling food, and Russian-speaking townsfolk went about their day-to-day business, seemingly oblivious to the misery all around them.

Danylo went up to the first market stall he passed. "How much for that?" he asked, pointing at a loaf of white bread.

"More than you have to pay for it," answered the man behind the stall, as he appraised Danylo's homespun clothes.

"What do you have that I could afford?" asked Danylo. And he unwrapped his precious bundle and drew out the silver spoon.

The man examined it with cold, appraising eyes. "I'll take

that for this," he said, and he held up a small loaf of the cheapest, blackest bread that he had.

Danylo was in no position to argue. He handed over the spoon and grabbed the bread, tearing off one chunk on the spot and devouring it. Almost immediately, he felt a little bit stronger. But Danylo considered how much he had paid for that one loaf of bread, and how little he had to buy more. He knew that he had to come up with a way to get to a safer place.

As days passed, Danylo became adept at stealing bread from the market stalls. He also learned how to evade the grasp of the Communist Party members who scoured the streets, looking for urchins like himself.

Most days, the comrades were content with keeping the ever-encroaching multitude of starving children away from the market stalls, but one day, their ambitions intensified. They methodically swept the streets and caught every last child. Danylo feared for his life as he and the others were herded into a vacant warehouse across from the train station. As the door was closed and bolted from the outside, darkness enveloped the sorry group. Most were too weak and exhausted even to protest. All around Danylo, little ones curled into balls and fell asleep. The windows of the warehouse had been blackened with paint, making it impossible to look out. But Danylo still had his knife with him, so he drew it from his belt and scraped a tiny bit of the window clean, just enough for a single eye.

What he saw amazed him. A Red Army officer was in the middle of the square at a makeshift desk. Behind him was a rack of what looked like Ukrainian folk outfits. The officer had a metal box and a sheaf of paper on the table in front of him. A lineup of city folk had formed. As the officer marked down something on the paper, he would hand each person what appeared to be money from the metal box, and then the person would walk behind the desk and choose a costume. What in heaven's name were they doing? Danylo wondered. Putting on a play? After more than a dozen people had chosen outfits, Danylo lost interest. Like the other inmates, he found a bare spot on the floor, curled up into a ball, and fell asleep.

He awoke with a start some time later. There was a horrible, frightening, and otherworldly sound outside. It was so awful that Danylo was almost afraid to look out, but his curiosity got the better of him. He crept back up to the peephole and looked out.

There, just thirty feet in front of him, was what could only be a train. It was like a fire-breathing monster, and he shook with fear as the huge creature screeched to a halt. Once his heart had stopped fluttering with fear, Danylo examined this odd contraption as best he could. It was made up of individual wheeled boxes, all linked together like sausages.

One of these boxes was a sleek unit, with huge glass windows on the side. Even from the warehouse, Danylo could see that the windows on the train compartment were either painted or papered over. Strange, Danylo thought. Perhaps it's to transport urchins?

Just then, a door opened on the compartment and a uniformed man jumped out. He fiddled with the lower part of the doorway until a set of metal steps appeared, reaching to the ground. Almost immediately, a number of well-fed adults stepped out of the doorway and onto the platform of the train station.

Danylo knew, just by looking at them, that these people were foreigners. They wore strange clothing, and many of them carried pads of paper and were writing in them, even as they were stepping down to the platform. There was also a Red Army officer mingling with the group.

As if on cue, a group of townspeople appeared. Danylo was shocked to see that these people were dressed in the Ukrainian folk outfits. They all looked healthy and well fed. One young girl walked up to the foreigners and presented them with the traditional welcoming of braided bread and salt. As this performance was being acted out, others set up a table in the square and placed an embroidered cloth over it. They motioned the foreigners to sit down at the table. Then the actors brought out bowls and platters filled with steaming food. Danylo could hardly contain his envy as he watched the well-stuffed foreigners stuff themselves even more. What was this all about?

Shortly after, the people got back on the train, and it pulled away. A few minutes after that, a party comrade came over to the warehouse, removed the bolt, and opened the door wide.

"Phew," the man muttered in Russian. "Don't you *khakhols* (an insulting term for Ukrainians) ever bathe?"

Danylo and the rest wandered out. Their lack of hygiene was the least of their worries.

As the days passed, other trains came in, but they carried goods, not people. Some of them were filled with wood and coal; some were empty. Danylo watched as children like him hopped into these compartments when the Communist Party members weren't looking. More often than not, the comrades would search the cars before they departed. It was the rare urchin who escaped this way. Danylo knew that he had to get on a train himself one day soon. Any place would be better than here.

Then one day, he saw his chance. The party members were sweeping the streets for every single child again, and so Danylo knew that another passenger train was coming. Would another charade also be performed? The comrades wouldn't dare search a passenger car for urchins; that would be too embarrassing for them, since urchins weren't supposed to exist.

He dashed away from the streets altogether, and hid on the outskirts of town. Then he waited for the train to appear. When it roared in, he skulked back into town, making sure to stay hidden. He needn't have worried. All attention was focused on the spectacle of rosy-cheeked "Ukrainians" and the delicious, steaming dishes they were serving.

The door to the train car had been left open, so Danylo waited until the uniformed man wasn't watching. Then he dashed inside. In a flash, he took in his surroundings. There were two rows of cushioned benches and a pot-bellied coal stove at the far end of the car. He hid himself quickly, behind the stove.

A few moments later, he heard a set of footsteps. He was afraid to look out to see if it was a Red Army officer who had followed him on to the train, or simply one of the passengers. He tried to stay still; he tried not to breathe.

The footsteps sounded louder and Danylo soon realized that a person was standing in front of the stove. A shiver of fear shot through him, and then he heard the voice of a young girl speak in Russian.

"They'll find you if you stay there."

Danylo was frozen with fear. He hoped wildly that somehow it wasn't him she was talking to; but the next thing he knew, a hand rested on his shoulder.

"I can see your shoulder as clear as day," she said. "It would be better if you hid under here."

Danylo dared to look out. A well-fed girl about his age stood before him. Her gloved hand pointed to a space underneath one of the benches. Then they could hear voices, close to the open door of the car.

"Hurry!" cried the girl.

Danylo scrambled from behind the stove and rolled under the bench. The girl shoved some luggage underneath the bench to hide him, and then she sat down on the bench above him.

How was it that she had been so willing to help him? Had this girl scraped a bit of paint off her own windows, and recognized the truth where her parents had not? How many others really knew what was going on in Ukraine, but preferred the charade?

Danylo settled himself under the bench and looked around. He noticed that one of the items she had shoved under was a wicker basket lined with a checkered cloth. He could smell sausage, and cheese, and bread. As the other passengers got onto the train, Danylo's stomach rumbled loudly. He prayed that no one could hear it.

Moments later, the train roared out of the station, and then Danylo could hear an official checking the passenger tickets. After he left, Danylo closed his eyes and tried to sleep, but the aroma of the food next to his nose was overwhelming. He reached in and drew out a long link of *kobasa*, a smoked sausage. Almost swooning with hunger, Danylo drew the knife out of his belt and cut off a piece of meat. He bit into it and chewed with pleasure. He took a few more bites and then put it back in the basket. As the hours passed and the memory of the wonderfully fatty *kobasa* filled his mind, he couldn't stop himself from reaching in and taking another bite. Before he knew it, the whole link was gone. He would have liked to eat the bread and cheese, too, but by sheer force of will, he stopped himself.

It was a good thing he did, because a few hours later, a hand reached down and picked up the basket, momentarily exposing Danylo to anyone who happened to look down. The girl quickly rearranged herself above him, though, covering him back up again.

"Rachel, you little imp," said a man's voice. "You've eaten all our sausage!"

"I'm sorry, Papa," said the girl. "I was starving, and it smelled so good."

"Next time, ask if someone else wants a bit, before you devour the whole thing," the man said in an exasperated voice.

"I will," she said meekly.

The train rumbled on, and night fell. Danylo drifted off to sleep, only to wake up with a jolt hours later, when the train was still. Eating all of that *kobasa* had upset Danylo's stomach and he was doubled over with pain. He had an urgent need to fart, but he was afraid that if he did that, he would wake the people sleeping in the compartment.

The car door was open again, and there were men smoking on the platform outside. Without giving much thought to a plan, Danylo rolled out of his hiding place and, on legs leaden and numb from being cramped up for so long, hobbled out the car door. A uniformed man on the platform tried to grab his collar as he sped past, but Danylo broke free. He ran and ran, as far from the train as he could get. Then, when his pain would let him run no farther, he collapsed on the ground in agony and let out one long, loud fart. He felt better immediately. Looking around, he saw that he was completely alone. It was the deepest part of night. He hugged his bundle to him and fell asleep.

He woke to the feeling of bright sun shining in through his eyelids. He tried to get up but realized that he was almost numb through with cold. He wriggled his arms and legs to get the circulation back and then stood up and looked around to see where he had landed. The train was long gone, and Danylo was in the middle of nowhere. Not a house, field, or village in sight, just mile upon mile of open steppe. Danylo walked back to the train tracks and waited for another train. In the days that he waited, he ate roots and grass and bugs. And he dreamed of the lovely *kobasa*.

When a train finally passed by, it didn't stop. Danylo had to run beside it and hoist himself onto an empty freight car. He was so hungry by the time the train pulled into a station that he decided to risk going outside, to see if he could find food. He was no sooner off the train when a Red Army soldier grabbed him by the collar.

"Where are you going?"

Danylo had already seen the fate of urchins who had been caught, so he thought fast for a plausible excuse. "I was visiting friends and am just on my way back home."

The soldier looked Danylo up and down; he didn't buy the story for a moment. "Come with me," he said. He took Danylo to a freight car that had been pulled off the tracks, and shoved him through the open door. It was filled with filthy and emaciated urchins. There was no food or water in the car, nor even a pot to pee in. The soldier locked the door behind Danylo.

Each day, a few children died. The doors were opened to remove the dead children, and the live ones were led out to relieve themselves. Food was brought in, on occasion, but never more often than every other day. Danylo saw that his legs were swelling and he knew that starvation was again setting in. He considered trying to escape on the daily visit to the lavatory, but he knew he wouldn't have the strength. His only hope was to lie still enough and hope that he was mistaken for dead.

He felt himself gripped by the ankles and hands and tossed on the top of a mound of corpses. He forced himself not to cry out. He had seen so many dead bodies in his short lifetime that it surprised him how upset he found himself to be. What kind of monsters were these comrades, who considered people like Danylo to be no more than rubbish to be thrown out?

The cart rumbled away from the freight car, and Danylo felt himself swaying back and forth, perched precariously on top of a mass of human bodies. The sweet, sickly smell of rotting flesh enveloped him as the cart pulled away from the train depot, away from the village, and into darkness. Danylo drifted off into an uneasy sleep.

The cart came to a jolting stop, and Danylo had to force himself to keep still. Suddenly, he felt the cart tip, and then he and the bodies tumbled out, into a pit. A gust of fresh air enveloped Danylo, and the smell of rotting was momentarily replaced with a sharp whiff of freshly-dug black earth. The scent brought back memories of his family farm. Each spring and summer, that same wonderful scent of rich, black earth was in the air for seeding and harvest.

The lovely scent was soon extinguished, as the weight of corpses from the bottom of the cart fell on top of him, covering him completely.

Danylo lay there amidst the dead for what seemed like hours. He was afraid to dig himself out in case the corpse collectors were still there, yet he was even more fearful of staying where he was. He knew that if he drifted into unconsciousness, he would suffocate. When he could wait no longer, he slowly burrowed his way to the top. He remembered that the commissars in his village sprinkled lye on the mass graves to make them deteriorate faster; so when Danylo sensed he was near the top layer of corpses, he gingerly flipped each body over, making sure not to touch the upper surface and risk burning from the lye. When he finally broke through, he was glad for his foresight. The sharp smell of lye hung in the air.

It was still dark, but Danylo could see that daybreak was close at hand. The dark of the night looked almost bright compared to the hellish darkness at the bottom of the pit. In the moonlight, Danylo looked at his hands and feet and was dismayed to see them ballooning out with starvation. He had very little time. If he didn't find something to eat, he would die.

He could see the silhouette of the huge mound of freshly dug earth. As his eyes adjusted, Danylo could also see that the pit had been dug in a farmer's empty field. He realized that he was standing in the midst of a potato field that had lain fallow for a year, but had partly reseeded itself. A few brave seedlings had grown wild and were beginning to rot. What madness was this? Farmers were starving to death in the midst of soil so rich that it practically planted itself.

The mound turned out to be the best place to look. As soon as he found the first potato, he scraped the dirt off it with his knife and then bit into it. The taste of juicy, raw potato filled his mouth. It tasted almost as good as the *kobasa* from the train. Once he finished the first potato, he dug out a dozen more and hid them in his shirt. His feet were still painfully swollen inside of his shoes, and his hands were so big that it took an effort to make them work. But he knew that the swelling would soon go down, now that he had eaten.

The most important thing, at this point, was to get away from the mass grave and hide before daylight. But Danylo also knew that the weather was changing. If he were to survive the winter, he would have to find warmer clothes. He turned back to the spot in the mass grave from which he had emerged. Here, the bodies covered with lye had been turned over, exposing the unmutilated corpses one layer down. Gingerly, Danylo stepped back in amidst the bodies and looked for warmer clothing. Ghostly faces of hollow-eyed children, and men and women old before their time, stared back at him. A sob caught in Danylo's throat as he stood there, hugging himself in sadness. Who mourned for these innocents, piled like so much rubbish in a farmer's field? Danylo vowed to himself to live, not only for his own sake, and for the memory of his family, but also as a tribute to those who died.

The dead were dressed in rags no better than his own, so he opted for quantity, removing several large threadbare coats, layering them one by one. He tied rags about his shoes, both for warmth, and to hold them together.

Then he wandered on weary legs, in the only direction he knew—away.

He wandered, delirious for days, subsisting on bites of potato. Once the potatoes were gone, he used his knife to dig through the frozen earth for roots and bark. When he found a set of train tracks, he followed them. Days later, they began to vibrate beneath his feet. When the train came, it moved slowly enough for him to jump into a freight car as it passed.

Days blended, one into another, as Danylo hopped from train to train. Sometimes he entered a boxcar that was already inhabited by one or two hollow-eyed children in rags.

He learned that the Famine ended at the River Zbruch. He heard tales of the few who had escaped the soldiers' bullets and crossed to the other side. What the other side held was a mystery, but Danylo was sure it had to be better. Otherwise, why would soldiers try to stop them from crossing?

He rode the rails in the direction of the River Zbruch. When he got there, it was a crisp, cold day and he could see soldiers posted amidst the trees along the icy banks. Danylo hopped off the boxcar and hid in the bushes before the train stopped. From his hiding place, he observed the soldiers' movements.

There was a cluster of Red Army soldiers by the station. Danylo watched as the train came to a halt. A soldier walked up to the boxcar he had just vacated and looked inside. Thank goodness he had decided to jump off early! Danylo darted from bush to bush, making his way downriver and away from the station. There were soldiers as far as he could see, but he had no choice but to keep moving. The river itself was almost completely frozen over in spots.

As he got farther away from the station, Danylo kept his eyes on the banks of the river. His biggest challenge was to remain hidden. The land beside the River Zbruch was largely clear, open, and covered with snow, so even his footprints would betray his escape.

During the day, he hid behind the scarce bits of brush that he found. He traveled under the cover of night, placing each step quietly and carefully. As he got farther away from the train station, he saw that there were slightly fewer soldiers, but they were still there. He also noticed that the soldiers paid particular attention to the areas of the river that were narrower, and to the parts that were more or less frozen over.

After days of traveling by night and hiding by day, Danylo could see the changes in the river. It had become much wider. His heart sank. How would he ever get across? As he continued, he saw a small island in the middle of the river. It was only big enough to hold about a dozen trees, but there was deep brush along the edges. Best of all, the river looked frozen right to the edge of the little island. It was getting darker, and Danylo had not seen a soldier for a few hundred yards. Should he take a chance?

Before he could think too carefully about it, he dashed down to the shore of the river and stepped upon the ice. It held firm. As he looked down at his feet, he saw other footsteps in the snow. Perhaps this was a sign of a successful escape? He kissed his parents' wedding rings for good luck, and then dashed out toward the island. He knew he would be in full view for hundreds of yards around: a black speck on the white ice. But what choice did he have?

When he was so close to the island that he could almost reach out and touch it, he heard a shot behind him. He felt a sharp pain in his shoulder. Danylo threw himself into a bush and rolled into the depths of the island as he heard more shots.

Suddenly, he heard a shrill scream. He lay, not daring to move, waiting for a shower of bullets to pierce his rags. He heard footsteps running away from him, and then another scream. He dared not look up.

From the corner of his eye, he saw a bone-thin woman running away from the island and back toward the land of famine. In her arms she held a bundle, stained with blood. Danylo realized that the woman and her child must have hidden on the island just before he had. He watched in horror as the grief-crazed mother ran up to the soldier and set the body of her dead child down at his feet. Then she threw herself at the soldier, pounding her fists and flailing her arms. The soldier was so surprised that he dropped his gun and grabbed her by the wrists.

Danylo didn't wait to see more. He scrambled to the other side of the island, then dashed across the ice to the other side of the river.

Danylo had no memory of the next few days. Weak with hunger and delirious from the throbbing pain in his shoulder, he somehow stumbled across the countryside toward freedom.

His next recollection was when he was safe. The village Danylo found himself in was much like that of his childhood, though slightly more prosperous. Most of the houses had thatched roofs, but some had tin roofs, and eaves troughs decorated with beautiful, swirling patterns punched into the metal.

The Krawchuk clan, who had adopted Danylo as their own, lived in a blue-washed clay cottage at the outer end of the village's only street. When Danylo had made it to the village, emaciated and near death, Anna Krawchuk was the first to notice him. She had been on her way to the well when she spotted a heap of rags not far from her door. She cradled him in her arms, as if he were her own child, and took him home. She nursed him back to health with sips of rich borscht and *kolach* (a rich, braided egg bread) dipped in honey.

The bullet had grazed the surface of his shoulder, creating a superficial gash about three inches long. His layers of rags had stuck together with oozing blood and pus. Anna cut away the cloth and the dried blood, cleaned the wound with an herb tincture, and then bound it with a cool, damp, bread poultice.

His teeth chattered so badly with cold and fever that Anna made a bed for him on top of the *pich* and bundled him in a down-filled comforter. For added warmth each night, she had her two sons sleep on either side of Danylo.

Danylo suffered days and days of delirium. The hand-painted border of flowers along the top of the whitewashed walls seemed to spring alive, their leaves stretching out to grab him. The red petals seemed to drip with blood. The delicate lace curtains on the windows fluttered innocently in the breeze by day; but at night they wavered like white-knuckled hands, thin to the bone, and fluttered as if in the last moments before death. Danylo clutched his parents' rings and prayed for deliverance.

As soon as he was strong enough, Danylo asked Anna to take him to the graveyard. She seemed to know instinctively what he wanted to do, and so she took along several small handmade candles. To get to the graveyard, they had to walk down the main street and through the centre of the village. They turned left at the *chytalnya* (reading room) and crossed over a footbridge, and then up a small hill. Even though it was winter, the cemetery seemed beautiful to Danylo. He envied the people who were buried here. They had died one by one, and each had been grieved for and prayed for individually. He wandered through the rows of gravestones, with Anna following a few feet behind. He methodically brushed snow off the stones as he went, and read each inscription carefully. When he came to one labeled Larissa, a sob escaped his throat.

He fell on his knees in front of the stone, and prayed for the baby sister he had lost. Anna took a few steps forward and gently placed her hand on his shoulder, murmuring prayers. Then she knelt down beside Danylo. She handed him a candle and a match. He set the candle on top of the headstone, and lit it. Then he prayed for the girl in the grave, but mostly he prayed for his own sister. He repeated his tributes until he had prayed for every one of the lost members of his family.

It was dark by the time they walked home.

Spring Harvest

LINDA MIKOLAYENKO

Sure can do a lot of damage to the crops,
    those gophers,
said Mr. Nicholson, sipping tea.
       farmer with a reputation
       had twenty thousand in the bank

1934 is going to be a bad year for them, they say
Municipality's paying one cent a piece.

Mike nodded.
      immigrant hired seven months
      for one hundred dollars

Up at five, Mike
fed horses milked cows
set out poison in the fields
plowed planted fed pigs

Sun set late on spring days

Gathered up dead gophers
cut tails and hind feet for proof
put them in a box

Up at five, Mike
fed horses milked cows
set out poison in the fields
plowed planted fed pigs

Gathered up dead gophers
cut tails and hind feet
added them to the box

No chance to cash them in

Mr. Nicholson, you goin' to town?
How about you take my gophers?

Sure, Mike.

Returning in his wagon
Mr. Nicholson holds out
two dollars and thirty-seven cents

Mike, you got those gophers from my farm.
You work for me. My daughter wants a coat.
How about I keep one dollar?

Sure, Mr. Nicholson, sure.
> *if he had a daughter*
> *he'd rather she wear sheepskin*
> *than rodent.*

*The Caruk sisters of Pine River—Mrs. Mary Krawchuk and
Mrs. Emily Zahidniak, taken in 1930*

1938

The Red Boots

MARSHA FORCHUK SKRYPUCH

My father, Marshall Forchuk, is a wonderful storyteller in his own right. He regales anyone within earshot with highly amusing and detailed incidents from his childhood and youth. "The Red Boots" is based on a story that I heard many times as a child. It's a slice of prairie homestead life in the late 1930s, during a prosperous lull after the Depression and before World War II.

Originally written in 1992, "The Red Boots" was my first children's story.

It was so cozy under the goose-feather *pyryna* (duvet)...was it really time to get up? But the smell of baking bread meant that Mama had already been up for at least an hour. I poked my head out and felt the shock of icy bedroom air. Through the darkness, I could see that my brother's bed was empty. Morning had arrived. And today was a special day!

I hopped out of bed, keeping warm by running on the spot. Without removing my white long johns and thick socks, I quickly pulled on a heavy woolen sweater. I was sure to freeze in the outhouse, so I made do with the pee pot under the bed, then stepped into my overalls and ran downstairs.

The Forchuk family, taken in the 1930s—from left to right: Marshall (Slavko), Steve (Stefan), Walter (Vlodyu), Olga, and Jean

"Good morning, Slavko," greeted Mama, smiling, as she cut *solonyna* (sowbelly) into thin strips. I splashed warm water on my face and hands from the reservoir in the massive wood stove, savoring the intense smell of baking bread. This stove was Mama's pride and joy—a four-burner with a double oven. The front and sides were finished in creamy colored enamel with red trim. It was the only stove I had ever seen that wasn't completely black. But then again, everything in our Innisfree house was so much nicer than what we had on the homestead at Lake Eliza. I looked at the white plastered walls in this kitchen and remembered the old walls, which were made of shaped logs, fitted and nailed together with hand-carved wooden pegs. The cracks had been filled with a plaster made of mud, cow dung, and straw. The floor had been hard-packed dirt. I gazed down at the gleaming red-and-white checkered linoleum I was standing on now.

The old house could have fit into this kitchen. I looked up at Mama, who was busy at her modern stove, and remembered the oven in Lake Eliza. It was made of clay. On top of the oven was a warm, sodded area where we children used to sleep. An arm's length away, my parents slept on a homemade wooden bed with a horsehair mattress.

"Slavko, you're asleep standing up," chuckled Mama, interrupting my reveries. "Hurry with the chores. You don't want to get Tato angry. Not today."

I looked up at the clock on the wall. Already it was 5:30! There was no time to waste. I walked out the kitchen door to the cold room. This was a narrow storage area that was as long as the house. We used this room to hang up our winter clothing. It always smelled faintly of cow manure.

There was a narrow, eighty-foot-deep pit with a trap door at one end of the room. We would throw ice down the pit all winter. It became our food freezer in the winter and our food cooler in the summer. Old Sam, the Métis, had brought our order of frozen fish just last week. Old Sam was a fixture in the area. All winter he drove his sleigh, piled high with frozen-solid fish, from farm to farm.

The trap door was open, so I looked down. My little sister Jean, blue-lipped and shivering, was struggling up the makeshift steps with a pail full of frozen fish. She was almost at the top, so I reached down and grabbed the pail from her.

"Does Mama know you were down there?" I asked her sternly.

"No," she replied, still shivering violently. "But I know she's pickling some of the fish today, and I don't want to waste any time. Not today."

I helped her close the trap door, and then she hurried into the kitchen, pulling the pail of frozen fish behind her.

I got my working coat off its hook, and with numb fingers I did up the buttons. My boots were nowhere to be seen, so I forced my feet into Jean's work boots. I found my own hat and gloves, and walked out the back door.

Vlodyu and Stefan were already heating up the metal water trough for the livestock. The winter nights were so cold that the water trough froze solid in a matter of hours. Stoking up the fire under the trough was the last thing we did each night, and the first thing we did each morning, because the cows would hurt their teeth if they tried to get a drink through the ice.

"So, Sleeping Beauty decided to wake up," said Vlodyu, giving me a dirty look.

"Why didn't you wake me?" I asked defensively.

"I tried. But you were dead to the world."

As I helped crack the ice on top of the trough, Stefan piled wood underneath. Vlodyu was heating dippers full of water, one by one, for the two newborn calves and their mothers in the barn. It was far too cold for the fragile creatures to risk going outside.

Tato and Mama had already milked the cows; so once all of the ice in the trough was broken up, I went over to help Tato separate the milk from the cream.

"The snow's not bad today," I commented to Tato with forced casualness. "Maybe we'll be able to take the car in to the hall tonight."

"Don't count on it, Slavko," replied Tato, looking out of the barn at the still-black sky. "These last few days, the wind has drifted snow over the roads. It wouldn't be safe to take the car."

I continued to help Tato in silent frustration. Why, for once, couldn't he see that getting to the hall early was important? All winter, the children from the neighboring farms would meet at our place on Sundays to practice the skits, dances, *tsymbaly* (hammer dulcimer), and *bandura* (a harp-like stringed instrument). Tato would remove the doors separating the living room and dining room to provide enough space to practice. Each Sunday during the winter, our house was the center of activity for the whole Ukrainian community. The actual concert was to be held tonight at Ukrainska Hall, and our farm was the farthest, a full twelve miles away.

Last Sunday night had been the dress rehearsal. We were the last family to arrive. As one of the youngest dancers, I always got stuck wearing a plain outfit. How I admired the older boys' fancy costumes—red leather boots, flowing blue pants, embroidered blouses, and red sashes. We younger boys had to make do with plain white pants and our own socks, pulled up to the knee, as imitation boots. Our shirts had almost no embroidery, and our belts were sometimes mere binder twine. I desperately wanted to wear a fancy costume like the older boys.

Last week, in preparation for the dress rehearsal, I had fashioned a pair of Cossack boots out of tar paper—not red, but at least black boots were better than plain white socks! I had barely started my dance when the tar paper boots began to tear apart. By the end of my first dance, bits of tar paper littered the stage. Nestor Shumach, the oldest in the little boys' group—resplendent in a pair of oversized red boots and using a housecoat belt as a sash—looked at me pityingly.

"Forget it, Slavko. Little boys are supposed to be in white."

Slowly, the performers and their parents put away the costumes and instruments for the night. Ivanko Chenyk had extinguished the fire in the big, potbellied heating stove, and put out all the lights. Tato was getting the horses and sleigh ready, and Mama was talking to Nestor's mother. As I took off the plain shirt and pants, I noticed that Nestor had left his fancy outfit carelessly piled on top of a wooden chest. The rule was first come, first serve. I knew that on the night of the performance, Nestor would get here before me. He lived two miles closer. But what if I could find a hiding place for my coveted outfit now? I looked around. The other children were either riding home already, or out on the stage, horsing around and waiting for their parents to stop chatting.

Where was a secure hiding spot? Behind the chest? Too obvious. Underneath? I strained, but the chest was too heavy; I couldn't lift it up.

What about underneath everything in the girls' chest? Nestor would never think of looking for his special outfit there! I carefully wrapped the red boots inside the blouse and pants, and tied the whole bundle securely with the housecoat sash. Shivering with satisfaction, I buried the package deep within the mound of girls' costumes.

"Slavko, hurry up!" It was Mama calling. I scampered down the stairs, trying hard to keep my face from grinning. And we started on our long journey home.

That was last week. Would the special outfit still be hidden? Would we get there before Nestor tonight? I could only hope.

"Slavko," Tato said sharply, breaking me from my daydream, "please answer me when I ask you something. How much wood do we have in the cellar?"

"We filled it up before supper last night," I answered.

"Good," he replied. "Go get your brothers; you can all shovel out the barn now."

Stefan had just finished making swill for the pigs—skim milk mixed with chopped oats—in the trough. Vlodyu led the cows out to eat and drink, and we all hurried into the barn to clean the manure out of the stables. We had to work fast so the cows' udders wouldn't freeze.

Once we had cleaned out the barn and got the cows back

in, we all headed to the house for breakfast. Olga was outside shoveling the last bits of snow off the porch. She followed us in. As we removed our outer clothes in the cold room, the smell of cow manure rose in steamy wisps. Tato held the kitchen door open, and we all filed in. At once, my nostrils were filled with kitchen smells—fried *solynena*, warm bread, and pickling fish.

Jean had covered the table with an oilcloth and set out bowls and plates for each of us. We had a hearty breakfast of Sunny Boy Cereal, bread, jam, and *solynena*. I wiped up the last bit of grease from my plate with a crust of bread, and I thought back to all the breakfasts we had eaten at our homestead back in Lake Eliza. Even during the Depression, we had a good breakfast each day. But I had been acutely aware of how little others had.

Rafts carrying starving children and their parents would float listlessly past our homestead, down the North Saskatchewan River. The sight of these poor beings was a torture to Mama, so she set up a stand with eggs and curdled milk at the edge of the river. We painted a sign that stated, in several languages, *Take what you need, but save some for the next person.* We would fill the stand twice a day. Homeless men—looking for food and a warm place to sleep in exchange for a bit of work—would wander from farm to farm. We always had two or three of them living in our barn, doing whatever odd jobs Mama could find for them.

As I swallowed the rest of my fat-drenched bread, I looked up at the kitchen clock. It was already 7:00! There were so many chores yet to do.

My brothers and sisters and I scurried around the farm, getting each chore done as quickly as possible. But we always had that sinking feeling that no matter how fast we were, we would still be the last ones to the concert. Tato did not believe in milking the cows too early. "It upsets their routine," he would say sternly. So even when all the work was done and supper eaten, we still had to wait until at least 4:00 p.m. to milk the cows and let them out for more water.

There was a knock on the door a few minutes after 4:00. It was Victor, Nestor Shumach's older brother. He had come to drive Olga to the hall.

"Can I please come with you?" I begged.

"No," replied Olga. "If I let you come, then Jean will want to come, and so will Stefan and Vlodyu. You can drive with Mama and Tato. They'll be leaving pretty soon, anyway." And with that, she left—a satisfied look on her face.

While the others milked the cows, Vlodyu and I got the horses and sleigh out of the stable. The sleigh was made of a twelve-foot-long grain box, which had been bolted onto sleigh runners. We piled oats into the sleigh.

Then we waited, and waited, and waited.

What was taking them so long with the milking? I ran into the house to check the clock. It was 5:00 already. The concert started at 8:00 p.m. sharp. Ukrainska Hall was twelve miles away, a good three-hour drive. Even if we left this minute, we might be late.

I ran into the barn to see how much was left to do. The cows were all watered and milked and back in their stalls.

"Hurry up, slowpoke!" I heard Tato call from outside. I hurried out of the barn to see everyone loaded into the sleigh and ready to go. Maybe we wouldn't be late after all.

Mama and Tato sat up front, with Jean between them. They were bundled in blankets. My brothers and I sat on top of the oats piled up in the sleigh. It was a cozy ride there, all bundled up in blankets and cushioned with oats.

Ukrainska Hall gleamed like a beacon in the darkness as we approached. There were so many sleighs there already that we knew the barn would be full. Our poor horses were going to have to wait for us in the bitter cold. We rubbed them dry, so their sweat wouldn't freeze, and then draped the blankets over their backs. Tato put down a big bundle of oats in front of each horse for them to munch on while we were inside for the concert.

The heat and light of Ukrainska Hall burst upon us as we entered. The warm air smelled of manure, wet wool, and sweat. The room was gigantic. There were enough benches set up for a hundred or more people. The stage, draped with elegant gold and crimson curtains, looked like something out of a book. On the walls, portraits of famous Ukrainians stared sternly down at me.

I hurried up to the change room, peeling off my coat and hat as I ran. Would the outfit still be hidden?

Olga was there, helping the dance teacher organize the younger children into their groups. She looked like a princess in her embroidered blouse and red skirt. Someone had braided her hair and wrapped it into a thick coil surrounded with a crown of paper flowers.

"Slavko," she said, "hurry up and get dressed. Your group is going on first."

I dashed over to the two wardrobe boxes. Looking over my shoulder to make sure I wasn't being watched, I quickly rooted through the remaining girls' costumes in search of the precious bundle. It wasn't there.

"Slavko, put these on fast. There's no time to lose." Olga tossed me a plain white shirt, without even a stitch of embroidery, and a plain white pair of pants. "I went through the boys' wardrobe box as soon as I got here," she said. "I know how particular you are about your costume. You've got the newest little boy's costume in the whole wardrobe. Not a tear or stain or anything."

Olga looked so proud of herself, I thought, as I sullenly dressed myself in the pure white outfit. If only I had thought to ask her to get my bundle out of the girls' wardrobe.

Then, Nestor Shumach swaggered into the change room, resplendent in *my* outfit—red boots, wide pants, embroidered shirt, and the beautiful bathrobe sash.

"Slavko," he said, "shouldn't you change out of your long johns? We're just about to go on the stage." I looked down at my white costume. It did look like long johns. The older dancers chuckled at his cruel joke.

Swallowing back tears of humiliation, I ran out of the room and searched the hall for Tato.

"I am not going to dance tonight," I announced in a trembling voice.

"Nonsense. You've looked forward to this night all winter," he said to me sternly, holding my chin in his hand so I had to look up at his eyes. "Besides, it would break your mama's heart if you didn't dance. Now go."

The musicians took their places in front of the stage. "Get up there," urged Tato. Through angry tears, I could see the blur of little boys, all dressed in white, as they lined up to get to the back of the stage. Nestor, in his colorful finery, was last in line. I fell in behind him and sullenly walked to my position on the stage.

The curtains opened and the musicians played our dance. I was in misery, but I went through the dance as if in a trance, not looking left or right. The audience was a blur. I couldn't tell where my parents were sitting.

The few minutes of the dance seemed like hours, but finally it was over. We all took our bows and listened to the thunderous applause of parents and relatives. Through the corner of my eye, I noticed that Nestor had stepped into the middle and was performing an extra little bow. I guessed that everyone was really clapping just for him.

As soon as the curtains closed, I ran off the stage and back up to the change room. I tore off that horrible white outfit and threw it into the boys' box. I pulled on my own clothing and got out of that room before Nestor and the other boys were even off the stage.

The older girls were dancing now. Olga looked beautiful, her finery flowing with each graceful movement. But I just wasn't in the mood to watch dancing anymore. I snuck out the back door of the hall and went to visit our horses. They were stomping the snow to keep their feet warm, and the blankets had fallen off. I carefully shook the snow out of each blanket and, one by one, placed them back on the horses. Then I got them some water.

The stillness of the frigid outdoors had a settling effect on me. I inhaled a deep breath and let it out slowly, watching the mist rise in the darkness. Then I walked back inside. Why should I let Nestor get the satisfaction of spoiling this evening? I pasted a smile on my face and walked right up the middle aisle, taking an empty seat in the front row.

I concentrated on looking like I was enjoying myself, even clapping to the music of the *hopak* (a popular traditional folk dance). With a start, I noticed that sitting right beside me was the new girl from school. Her name was Natalka, and she was very pretty. As the *hopak* ended, I looked over and gave her a timid smile.

"I saw you dancing up there," she said, loud enough to be heard over the applause. "You're a good dancer."

"Thank you," I replied, blushing.

"You were lucky, too," she continued. "I felt embarrassed for that poor Nestor."

"What do you mean?"

"He must have arrived late. He was the only one who didn't get the proper outfit."

I blinked in surprise. The room felt warmer, friendlier.

"Yes," I said, grinning. "Poor Nestor."

Violin

SONJA DUNN

When my father, Volodymyr Serotiuk, came to Canada from Ukraine in 1926, work was scarce even though he was a professor of Ukrainian language and culture. One way to earn a dollar was to play at Saturday night dances, zabavas, in people's kitchens. His violin was his treasure. The kitchen table was removed, chairs were set up against the walls, and everyone danced waltzes, polkas, kolomykas, and arkans. This was an affordable form of entertainment for many immigrants. Whiskey and beer were served.

Ukrainian musicians, 1970s

In the dusty old shop
    hidden behind Toffey Alley
    his arthritic hands
    slide over her curved body.
Her warm brown form
    responds to his tender caress.
After fifty years of playing her
    it will be crying time
    to say goodbye.
In his ageing heart
    he knows
All of her will still be his;
    her slender neck
    responding to his fingers
    her frame, seemingly fragile
    belying her strength.
Now, finely tuned
    she lets him
    pluck her taut strings.
In years past,
    the horsehair wildly flying
    from her bow
    she hummed waltzes, polkas
    dirges, arias

"Och skrypotcho skrypotcho*
  Little violin, gentle violin,
  for half a lifetime
  I earned my meager living
  on you,
  playing songs of joy, romance, and
  melancholy.
  What diversions they were,
  in depression years!"
In urban kitchens
  fiddler's little daughter
  sits half asleep
  in a chair pushed against the wall
  the floor cleared for dancing.
If she could only relive one hour
  of that precious time
  long ago;
  the dancers, the tunes
  forgotten by all but her.

Skrypotcho is the diminutive of *skrypka*, or violin

1930 to early 1940s

A Song for Kataryna

LINDA MIKOLAYENKO

The author's aunt, Michalina—
the real "Kataryna"

How could someone just disappear? "A Song for Kataryna" was inspired by my own questions about what had happened to a relative who disappeared long before I was born. In families and in society, violence, mental illness, deportation, and atrocities toward civilians in war are often sources of pain and shame. They are not always well documented. While many of my questions remained unanswered, in my search, I discovered that I was still able to establish a relationship with the person my heart longed to call "Auntie."

This story was written as a tribute to my aunt, and to all the women whose dreams for a better future in a new land were met with disillusionment and tragedy. Unfortunately, even today, the dreams of immigrant women are still often dashed.

*N*o one sang *Veechnaya Pamyat* (Eternal Memory) for Kataryna.

When I was a child, my father told me, "She disappeared." I believed him without question. After all, in the stories of my childhood, disappearing could take on a romantic meaning. In one legend in particular, "The Eternal Bride," the beautiful Olena disappears when she uses her talent for magic to be reunited with her one true love. When I was a child, Kataryna, too, could have disappeared by magic.

But then, when I was a teenager, my father told me, "She disappeared during the war"—as though that explained everything. I knew that unspeakable things had happened during the war, and we never spoke more about it then.

Now, when I ask him about Kataryna's disappearance, my father's eyes mist over, and his throat catches. I don't ask any more questions—at least, not of him. But the questions do not go away.

Who was Kataryna? It's odd how I've always referred to her as my father's sister. Never as my Aunt Kataryna. Her name just doesn't evoke the images that his other sisters do. They were my aunts. I can see my Auntie Marusia, sitting on a stool next to the stove in her kitchen, her gray hair held atop her head by a hat crocheted from strings salvaged from flour bags. I loved my aunt, Sister Josaphata, whose convent name and starched white habit were much too severe for her twinkling eyes and the dimples in her generous cheeks that matched her generous heart. Even my Auntie Sophia was my auntie, although I only knew her through her letters—letters that told me more about the climate and economic conditions of her country than they did about her. *It is a cold winter,* she would write. *We chopped down the cherry tree.*

No, Kataryna was always my father's sister—the one who disappeared during the war. For the longest time, the closest thing I had to a picture of her was a photo of a photo of a girl in a floral print dress with buttons down the front. My brother had taken a blurred snapshot of a collage of round-faced siblings, which hung on the wall of the Old Country home. The picture only added more mystery to this obscure person in my family's past.

When I think back on the few stories about her that my father had shared with me over the years, she comes to me as an ordinary girl, in an ordinary large, poor family in Ukraine. She was only two years older than my dad. He tells me they shared a pair of shoes. He describes her glee when he hurt his foot during an afternoon of antics. It swelled too much for him to put on his shoe, so she got exclusive use of the shoes until his foot healed.

She was nineteen or twenty—I don't even know her exact birth date—when my grandparents decided to immigrate to Canada. Auntie Marusia had already joined her husband here, but Auntie Sophia had just married and wanted to stay behind in the family home in the village of Sady, which means "orchards." By the spring of 1930, however, most of the land had been sold, and my grandparents and seven children left Sady for Canada. As their horse-drawn wagon pulled away from their thatch-covered house, in the early hours of the morning, my father shed so many tears that he vowed he would never cry again.

He describes Kataryna as being a gentle, sensitive girl. What was the depth of her emotion as she said good-bye to all the friends and family who had gathered to see them off? I wonder what Kataryna thought as they sailed across the Atlantic on the SS *Albertic*. Was she excited about the possibilities in a new country? My dad says she was a beautiful girl. I sometimes allow myself to fantasize about an onboard romance, even though all the romantic love scenes in Ukrainian folk songs take place in cherry orchards. In that Ukrainian legend of "The Eternal Bride," Olena turns herself into the first blossoming cherry tree and her true love is turned into a golden cloud of bees, so that they could forever share the gift of love. I, myself, have always dreamed of going to Ukraine in the springtime, when the cherry trees are in bloom.

Perhaps Kataryna thought that she was leaving one romantic image behind, only to replace it with another. But whatever fantasies about a better life in Canada Kataryna may have had, they must surely have been shattered soon after her arrival at the port of Québec. They would have to travel on the train for days to get to Winnipeg. Then they would wait at the Immigration Center with countless other families while my grandfather arranged to settle on a farm. Times were tough for newcomers on the prairies in the thirties. My father says he went to night school for a short time to learn some English. I wonder if Kataryna did as well. In any case, by 1932, she headed north to seek work in the mining town of Flin Flon. This is where the mystery begins.

Just a few months later and accompanied by a nurse, Kataryna traveled by train to Brandon, Manitoba. She was admitted to the mental hospital there. I'm told she had had a nervous breakdown. I was not satisfied with that diagnosis when I heard the story and thought that it would be a simple matter to get access to her medical file. I wrote to the person in charge of the records, but was surprised and frustrated to receive this reply:

I have tried to locate the person you were searching for. Unable to locate a file for anyone by that name. A check of the master index came up empty, as I did a review of the logs for that time frame.

I submitted several versions of the spelling of the name, but that didn't help. It's as though she had never existed. Yet, I know she was there. My father went to visit her several times. On one occasion, he brought some apples and gave one to her and one to another patient. As they munched on the apples, they chatted. "Has father paid off the farm yet?" she enquired. Suddenly, an apple core flew at my dad. The patient next to Kataryna had thrown it at him. Kataryna looked at her incredulously. "What's the matter with her?" she asked. *"Vona shcho doorna?"* (Is she crazy?)

Was Kataryna crazy? How did she end up in that hospital? Perhaps it was during one of those visits that my father formulated his theory. "She was a beautiful girl. Some boys wanted to take her to a show in Flin Flon. Two of them started to fight with each other. She got scared," he says.

Had witnessing a violent fight been too traumatic for her? Uncle Andrew didn't think so. One day he shared with me his theory. It was based on a conversation he had had with someone who had worked in Flin Flon at the time. Uncle Andrew had a chance encounter with this guy who boasted, "Yeah, we gave this one girl some Spanish fly*, then we all had a turn with her."

My uncle's voice filled with emotion as he recalled the conversation. "When I heard his story, I got angry all of a sudden, and I told him, 'That's my sister you're talking about!' Of course I shouldn't have said that, because then he shut up; and I missed my chance to find out for sure."

I wonder what kind of treatment Kataryna received at the hospital. The language barrier would almost certainly have prevented her from getting any meaningful therapy. It may have even interfered with a proper diagnosis. I suspect shock therapy was common practice then. I have no idea what that would have done to her mind.

---

*
Spanish fly is the term for a toxic substance which consists of the dried, crushed body of the green blister beetle known as *Lytta vesicatoria*, or the Spanish fly. It was mistakenly considered an aphrodisiac, and often given to women without their knowledge.

I do know, now, that her stay in the hospital cost a lot of money. Her parents had not paid off the farm yet, and they certainly could not afford the $140 hospital bill. She wasn't a Canadian citizen yet. The government ordered her deported. I can imagine what Kataryna's mother must have felt. No wonder my grandmother tried hiding her passport in the desperate hope it would prevent Kataryna's deportation. Of course it didn't.

When I got my first job in Ottawa, after university, I went to the Immigration Department to see if I could get her records. While they were able to provide evidence of her arrival in Canada, they told me they did not have deportation records for that time.

But Kataryna was certainly deported in 1934. The trip back on the boat must have been completely different from the previous one. Had Auntie Sophia not agreed to look after her she would undoubtedly have ended up in an asylum. Instead, Kataryna returned to her family home. For her own protection, the door was secured and bars were put on the window.

I don't know much about the following years. Auntie Sophia was a seamstress. Maybe Kataryna helped her sort buttons. Maybe she cooked meals. Maybe she sat all day and stared into space. I suspect that if any of the letters that Auntie Sophia had written to my grandparents during that time were still around, they would have given us a glimpse of her life.

Then one day in 1943, my grandparents received a letter informing them that Kataryna had disappeared. I can just imagine their grief. But what exactly had happened? What I wouldn't do, to set eyes on that letter. Yet maybe it contained more questions than answers. It was, after all, during the war. The Nazis were in Ukraine. Jews and "undesirables" were being rounded up. It seems that one day, when Auntie Sophia was out; Kataryna had escaped from the confinement of their home, never to return. Did she end up on a train to a concentration camp? Or was she shot in a massacre?

When my father visited Ukraine in the 1960s, he went to the site of a mass grave near the family home. I don't imagine he sang *Veechnaya Pamyat*. *Veechnaya Pamyat* is a refrain sung at funerals, memorial services, and at gravesides during the *panakhyda* (service for the dead).

In all my questions, Kataryna's memory is eternal. In all of my wondering, her memory is eternal. The mystery of Kataryna haunts me. On a holiday in the Caribbean one winter, I woke up in the middle of the night. I couldn't get back to sleep. Images of Kataryna's plight kept going through my mind. I imagined this scene:

Kataryna is walking down the village road, happy to be out in the fresh air. A hand suddenly grabs her. She turns to face the glare of the buttons on the uniform of a German soldier. His voice commands her to come with him. She resists. He tightens his hold on her dress. One of her buttons snaps off and falls on the ground. She struggles to reach down and pick up the button. The soldier grabs her roughly.

"My button!" she screams. "I have to pick up my button! My sister will be mad at me if I lose it!"

"Are you crazy?" says the soldier, and he drags her into the cherry orchard.

Kataryna closes her eyes. All she sees is buttons. The dark buttons on the rough shirts of the miners. The white buttons on the lab coats of the hospital staff. The buttons in the jars by her sister's sewing machine. The buttons on the soldier's uniform.

Kataryna never opens her eyes again.

In the morning, I tell my husband, "For our next overseas trip, we're going to Ukraine." I need to go to that orchard and sing *Veechnaya Pamyat* for my Auntie Kataryna. Then perhaps my soul can rest in peace.

Memories of Volodymyr Serotiuk's Birthday

SONJA DUNN

Sometimes, riding on a train
I think of you in the thirties
and can hardly keep from crying

From left to right, standing: Phillip Turkewich, Alice Woloshyn, Joseph Turkewich. Seated: Alice Woloshyn. Taken at family homestead near Winnipeg Beach, Manitoba, in the early 1930s

We were a carousel
governed by an out of whack calliope
gypsying
from Toronto to Geraldton
to Fort Frances
to Timmins
to Kenora
to Port Arthur-Fort William
to Sudbury
to Coniston
to Rouyn-Noranda
then back to Toronto

Always back to Toronto
where we had to leave the baby Mama had.
Standing six four
a stately hussar
wearing spats, watch chain and fedora
you held my skinny six-year-old hand.
We were a pair
riding the rails.

Mama died in thirty-seven
left me with you.
"Poison in the born parts," you told me.
The Catholic Children's Aid
said a man couldn't look after a little girl
properly
but we fooled them
didn't we
and ran away together.

They got Ronnie though.
He was only two days old.
"Some good family
will adopt the baby," Miss Jeffrey pronounced.

"Vee Ukrainians
no let people adopt our babies.
Vee no sign avay cheeldren," you said.

And we never did.

1943 to 1945

Auschwitz: Many Circles of Hell

STEFAN PETELYCKY

*During World War II, I joined the Organization of
Ukrainian Nationalists and fought both the Nazis and the
Soviets. "Auschwitz: Many Circles of Hell" is an excerpt
from my memoir,* Into Auschwitz, for Ukraine, *which
was published by Kashtan Press in 1999. This account
describes what happened to me and other Ukrainians in
the Nazi concentration camps where we were imprisoned.
I was determined to put this account on the record, before the
last of the Ukrainian victims of the Holocaust fade away.
Our sufferings have been ignored or denied far too often.*

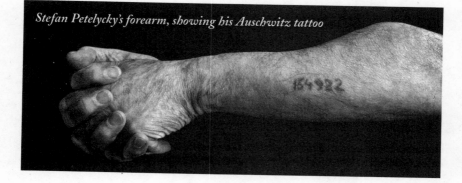

Stefan Petelycky's forearm, showing his Auschwitz tattoo

The number 154922 is tattooed on my forearm. I got the tattoo at Auschwitz. I spent more than sixteen months in the most infamous of the Nazi concentration camps. Then I was sent to Mauthausen, and from there to Ebensee. I saw things I can never forget, even if I wanted—that faded blue tattoo won't let me. I survived the Holocaust. I know all that I need to know about it. I was there. I remember. I can never forget. No one should ever doubt that the Nazis exterminated millions of people.

Ukraine lost more of its people than any other European country during the Second World War. Nazi propaganda characterized Ukrainians and other Slavs as *untermenschen*, subhumans who were slated for enslavement or extermination. For most Jews it was worse; no matter where they lived in Europe, they were, almost without exception, targeted for extermination and murdered in the millions.

While Jews were being targeted in Europe, Ukraine was also being depopulated. Its citizens were killed or carted away as slave laborers. Its rich natural resources were exploited for the benefit of the Third Reich. The Nazis imagined that they were a superior Aryan race, and they prepared to colonize Ukraine by murdering its inhabitants. Millions of Ukrainians were murdered. I saw some of this with my own eyes.

No European country was without its Judases, just as no people were without their blessed martyrs. I remember how, in 1943, it was a Pole who collaborated with the Gestapo and denounced me to the Nazis for aiding the Ukrainian resistance. He personally started me on my descent through the many layers of Nazi hell. In 1945, however, another Pole pulled me away from the open doors of the crematorium in Ebensee. He rescued me from the oven that, only days earlier, had burned up the mortal remains of my best friends. So when I think back to those years, I think of the one Pole as a Judas and of the other

Pole as a savior. I cannot think of all Poles as my enemies, nor of all Poles as my friends. Some were good; some were bad. Most just wanted to survive.

I reject those accounts of the Holocaust that seem to be intent on vilifying entire nationalities as collaborators, while portraying other peoples only as victims. I was anti-Nazi and still am. Yet even though I am a Holocaust survivor, I have never been anti-German. Not all Germans were Nazis. We must never hold the Germans of today responsible for the sins of their forefathers.

I was sent to Auschwitz because I was a Ukrainian nationalist. I was willing to fight for Ukraine's independence and, if need be, to die in the struggle. Many, like me, were sent into Auschwitz because they fought for Ukraine. Few survived. This is my story. It is also theirs.

On 1 October 1943, I entered Birkenau, sometimes known as Auschwitz II. That was the day on which I stopped being Stefan Petelycky and became number 154922.

The sun was setting when our transport arrived. I stepped out of a boxcar and into hell. Weedy fields stretched out before us, as far as I could see, and barking guard dogs were everywhere. We were ordered to form ranks, then to stand at attention while guards armed with submachine guns stood watch over us. An officer—the death's head insignia on his cap—came over and said to us that the sick, cripples, and anyone who was weak from the trip could take a ride by truck. Some poor souls took them up on the offer. That was the last we saw of them.

As we moved farther into the compound I could see clusters of wooden barracks in the distance, and above them, silhouetted against the evening sky, what appeared to be smoke stacks rising up out of brick buildings. Dark smoke was curling out of them. I gave no thought to them.

None of us knew what the Nazis were doing in Birkenau.

I was half-dead when I got there. I had been held for some four months—starved and tortured by Gestapo interrogators. I had not had anything to eat or drink for many hours. I had just got out of a boxcar that was full with many other men who were in similarly bad shape, or worse. Some were dead. We were all in terror. I took a look around, and I knew that this was the end. Why complain when they herded us off that cattle car and roughly tattooed us all? I saw one fellow, Petro Boian, who resisted. They just beat him senseless and tattooed him anyway. He ended up being number 154415, despite his protest, and he got a beating on top of that, all within minutes of clambering out of the box car.

I became a number, without a whimper.

Silent compliance seemed normal, given where we were. I had just about abandoned all hope of survival by the time I got there. I was truly indifferent when I got the tattoo that would define my life in so many ways. I was dazed, hungry, exhausted, and it was almost dark. We had heard about these camps, but nothing, as I have said, was certain; nothing was clear. Of course, we had seen that the Jews had been forced to live in ghettos. We had heard that there had been killings in the ghettos. Still, before I got to Birkenau, I had no real idea of what was going on in the camps. When I finally got there and took one look at the smoke stacks, the electrified barbed-wire fences, the watchtowers, the barracks, and the thousands of people lined up and forced to stand, barely clothed, in the cold autumn air, I felt certain that I was coming to the end of my life.

We were led along a fence where we could see inside the death camp. A group of prisoners staggered by. They were emaciated and exhausted. All were wearing striped uniforms. I remember noticing that one prisoner's head was drenched with blood. When I saw these prisoners, I was suddenly and utterly overcome with fear. To my astonishment, a little farther on, we passed a small group of Gypsies playing on musical instruments. They looked healthy by comparison with the other inmates. Some of them, men and women, were even dancing around; others were fighting among themselves. Large black crosses were painted on the backs of their fatigues.

After we had marched through the main gate, some SS men counted us. Behind them stood a row of strong, healthy prisoners who wore red and yellow armbands and had green triangles on their fatigues. They had thick clubs in their hands and rushed us along on the double. *"Tempo! Tempo! Los! Los!"* (Speed it up!) They beat anyone who failed to move quickly. They targeted anyone who showed even the slightest defiance or pride with many more blows. Their intention was to crush our will from the outset—that's how we newcomers were welcomed into hell and shown how we could expect to exist.

Then we were searched. Anyone found hiding anything of value was punished with twenty-five strokes. We were shepherded by lackeys, who clubbed us through the registration process and taunted us, making these first few hours of our introduction to Birkenau a torment. I noticed that some of them were adept at pocketing the valuables they found in our ranks and they would trade a piece of bread for a piece of jewelry or gold that a prisoner had kept hidden in the vain hope that they could use it in the future. Some newcomers were so hungry that it seemed fair to give up a piece of gold for a chunk of stale bread.

We had become numbers, and that is all that we would ever be in Auschwitz. We were systematically stripped of our possessions, our identities, and our hope. Everyone tried to save some small thing—some personal item that could remind him of a different existence and cheer him up. But we were allowed to keep nothing. I remember how malicious they were about it, grinning and joking as they stripped us bare. They laughed as they told us that it was their job to get us acquainted with our new home, a home which we would only leave through the crematoria chimneys.

We were driven into a cramped space between two lines of barbed wire, crowded together, and then sorted out and sent to different barracks. I could see that other Ukrainians, other members of the OUN (Organization of Ukrainian Nationalists), were there with me. Later, I learned that at least 150 Ukrainian political prisoners were already in Auschwitz. Now they were joined by me, Bohdan Kachur, Ivan Lahola, Mykhailo Lahola, Vasyl Lesiuk, Lohyn, Myroslav Tatsii, and Mykhailo Yaremko.

I was assigned to Barracks 4. A Jewish *kapo* (overseer) greeted us by bellowing out that he knew we Ukrainians were all policemen from Lviv. He yelled out that he and the other Jews would soon make certain that we were all dead. We were then marched out into the cold night. Until 2:00 a.m., we were forced to carry soil over rough ground to an area near the kitchen, where we filled in a hole. Since we were given no tools to work with, we had to use our jackets to carry the earth. Our bare feet were soon bloody. Finally, exhausted, we were allowed back into the barracks. Four men shared each bed. One of the men I was with was Bohdan Kryzhanivskyi. He had been printing underground literature against the Nazis until he was caught. Later, he would try to escape by jumping into one of the ditches that surrounded part of our compound. But he was discovered and beaten to death.

The next morning I saw that several dozen other newcomers had died during the night. We were herded into the morning cold like sheep, and taken to a bathhouse where our heads and faces were shaved. After that we were issued some threadbare underwear, tin plates, and spoons. These utensils became precious possessions. Then we were lined up again—this time for soup made from turnips. I had barely eaten for some three days, and I remember that the turnip soup tasted delicious.

Then we were moved to another barracks, under quarantine. We were supposed to learn the rules of camp life in that quarantine barracks, to adapt to our new circumstances or die. Some of those who came with me died.

I doubt I would have survived if I had been left in Barracks 4. But five days later, we were moved to Barracks 7, thanks to the intervention of another Ukrainian, Bohdan Komarnytskyi. He was one of the old-timers, with Auschwitz tattoo number 33. He knew the ropes; he was a survivor. He had friends among the German *kapos* and knew the block leader. The Nazis assumed Komarnytskyi was a Pole, but we knew he was a Ukrainian. They had picked him up in Cracow. He had been one of the builders of Auschwitz, erecting the barbed-wire fences that would imprison him and so many others. At any rate, he realized that if we remained in Barracks 4, we would suffer a lot, for the Jewish *kapo* there was a bully who hated Ukrainians and who would have ensured that we were brutalized.

As an old hand, Komarnytskyi also taught us the skills we needed in order to have a chance of survival. He explained that we were no longer individual human beings. We were all numbers. We had to memorize our numbers. They were stitched onto our jackets and pants and, of course, tattooed on our forearms. We must be humble and self-effacing, and do only what everyone else did. We must not dwell on what the next day might bring. We must live for the moment, take every opportunity to scrounge for food, and never attract the attention of the *kapos* or the SS men. He didn't hold out much hope for any of us, he said, but if we did everything he told us, we might live at least a little longer. Some of us learned these rules and survived. Komarnytskyi did too.

I remember the first *appell*, or roll call. The gong rang out, and we had to rush to the parade square. Lackeys clubbed us all the way. One older man fell behind and arrived late. The guards beat him senseless. Then they bound his hands and feet and tied him to a stake. They lifted him up and dropped him to the ground, torturing him for all of us to see, wracking his limbs. The sight was too much for us newcomers. Some tried to run away; they jumped up on to the barbed-wire fences. They were electrocuted on the spot. One prisoner, an amazingly strong man, grabbed the wires and vaulted over the fence. The SS guards shot at him. An SS woman in the field outside the wire finally killed him. In the panic of these events, the crowd of newcomers had scattered. The SS restored order by threatening to continue shooting until we were all dead.

When we had assembled again, it became obvious that two of our fellow inmates were now missing. We were forced back into our barracks, and a search was held. No sooner had we settled in than a shout came, "Get up!" and out we went again to the square. The Nazis counted us again, comparing the numbers on our badges to the tattoos on our flesh, trying to determine which numbers had gone missing. Then we were sent back into the barracks again.

Just as many of us were beginning to get to sleep, exhausted after our long journey and the terrors we had already witnessed, the command came again—"Get up!"—and we ran out to the parade square. Covered in blood, frightened, cowering before us, were the two prisoners who had tried to escape. They had been hiding in a canal. Now, in front of all of us, they were tied up, fixed to a flogging stool, and beaten to death.

A young man standing beside me watched and wept. "They are killing my brother!" he cried. The poor lad was also a Ukrainian, from Berezhany.

I stayed in Barracks 7 at Birkenau for about another week. It was a mixed barracks, housing Jews, Poles, and Ukrainians—all of them trying to survive. After that first week, we were marched over to Block 11 in old Auschwitz. There were twenty-nine of these blocks in all. They had been used as housing for Polish border troops before the war. Each block had two accommodation levels and a small storage attic above. We were on the top floor, which was almost entirely populated by Ukrainians. I noticed that there were quite a few more SS men guarding us.

There were also quite a few Jewish *kapos*, dressed in black outfits, better fed than the rest of us, who did a lot of killing. Many of them belonged to a special formation known as the "Canada Commando." They sorted out the belongings of incoming prisoners, taking everything that was of value to the Third Reich's war economy, leaving only the naked men, women, and children, many of whom were then gassed. The *kapos* had many opportunities to steal, which they did, not that it helped most of them in the long run.

A lot of Soviet POWs were in the camp at this time, including a large group of Ukrainian women. They were housed in Block 11, two floors below us. We could sometimes hear them singing Ukrainian songs at night. The singing went on for about three weeks, and then it stopped abruptly one night. The next day we heard that they had all been taken away and shot. Only the empty cellar floor and the echo of their songs were left in our minds.

After three weeks, we were moved again, this time to Block 17 in the central compound. We marched in our clogs through the gate that was crowned with an iron sign, *Arbeit Macht Frei* (Work Shall Set You Free). I knew what that message really meant. The only way to set yourself free was to let them work you to death. That way you could escape through the chimney of the crematorium.

Even so, we all tried to survive. We *Banderivtsi*, as we were known because of our allegiance to Bandera's faction of the OUN, got together. We began trying to take care of each other and of other Ukrainians, too—as much as possible. For example, we tried to get our comrades jobs in the camp laundry, for that wasn't as hard a job as being assigned to a road construction crew. I worked at the heavy labor site, and I knew what it was like. We were forced to work fast, and the food was bad and scarce. Many of us fell ill and died every day. Our guards would march us out of the camp in the early morning, and we would spend the day building a road. We worked on it almost to the end of January 1944. You can imagine how difficult it was for men without proper tools—barely clothed and malnourished—to build a road in the late fall and early winter. We did anything we could to survive. We even stole empty cement bags to line our clothes for insulation. If we were caught we would get a beating. Imagine, a bad beating just for stealing a paper bag. Even so, we built that road, and we did a pretty good job of it.

At the end of a long day, we marched back to camp, passing under the *Arbeit Macht Frei* sign again. We were checked by the SS guards at the gate, to make sure that no one was smuggling anything into the camp and that we were all there. If the figures didn't match, we would be called out on parade and counted, over and over again, until all discrepancies were accounted for. We were ciphers, numbers without importance. The figures had to add up twice a day, at roll call in the morning and at roll call at night. The Nazis, I learned, were accountants of flesh, counters of corpses. We were nothing to them but so many work units, to be used up as they needed and then burned like trash.

My next job was in the SS kitchen. That was a good place to work. Most of the men who worked there were ethnic Germans—*Volksdeutsche*—although there were a few Russians and Ukrainians. No Jews worked there. My job was to move foodstuffs by cart from a storage area to the kitchen, as needed. I thought I finally had a chance to survive. If you were lucky enough to work near food, there was always a chance of swallowing an extra morsel to keep yourself going. But I wasn't there very long. When one of the *Volksdeutsche* was caught trying to escape with the assistance of the Polish underground, we were told, they immediately dispersed all of us. I ended up working in the laundry's washing room. At least it was warm and sheltered. There were Jews working there. They were from Poznan and were quite friendly. I worked with them until I was evacuated from Auschwitz, on 19 January 1945. The Soviets overran the camp on 27 January 1945.

I never participated in anything having to do with the mass murder of Jews or others at Auschwitz or anywhere else. But I did catch a glimpse of a particularly vile corner of the inferno. I had been cast into it on a day in the fall of 1944. The SS took me and six other men into the woods. When they told us to move out, I thought it was all over for me, that they were taking us to the woods to execute us. Instead, they made us load cut wood onto trucks and drive it to Birkenau, where the bodies of Jews who had been transported from Hungary were being burned. I had no idea of what they wanted to do with that wood until we got there.

We came to a large cement-lined trench, a hungry maw into which liquid fuel had been poured. Other prisoners then threw in the bodies of the Hungarian Jews who had been gassed soon after their transport arrived.

The stench of roasting flesh was incredible. We could see that these were the same Hungarian Jews who had arrived in Auschwitz in September or October 1944, most of whom were executed immediately or shortly after their arrival. I remember seeing thousands of pieces of luggage, piles of clothing, and other personal items. Seeing these pyramids of possessions made me think that I was a witness to the Final Judgment. I know it may sound strange today, but we often found ourselves thinking that we were no longer in this world, that we had somehow moved into a place that was closer to Hades than to Heaven, and that the world we dimly remembered no longer existed. That is how people existed in Auschwitz. Yet, at almost the same time, we would try to focus on the essential business of getting a little more bread, another ladle of what passed for soup, or a scrap of anything that could keep us alive. We survived as scavengers. We ate whatever came our way. We took food and clothing from those who had died, to give ourselves an extra chance to live. The will to live is remarkably strong.

The death and the brutality were soul-destroying. How long can a man or woman watch others die and remain unmoved? We cannot steel ourselves completely against the reality of what we are living, unless we give up and become, in effect, disembodied. When that happened to a person, we knew they had no will left to live. They lapsed into a kind of non-existence and, having given up, they soon died or were killed. We called anyone who had reached that state a *musulman* (walking corpse), a lost soul who was still walking among us, but who had the vacant look of someone who was already gone. To watch these zombies fading away, dissipating like shadows, was perhaps the most unnerving sight of all. You would get to know someone and learn something about him, and then, sometimes for no reason that you could understand, your new-found friend would just give up and their humanity would start to dissolve. There was nothing we could do to save such people. They simply lost the will to live, and died. Before Auschwitz, I did not believe that a person could give up hope and die. Yet that happened. People died because, deep inside, they had come to believe that life had no meaning, no purpose, and that there was nothing to life, except the horrors that the Nazis imposed. I was, and am, a man of faith, a Ukrainian Catholic. I believed in God and in a personal Savior, Jesus Christ. I know that my faith in God and the aid of my OUN comrades helped me survive.

On 7 January 1945, a group of us decided that we would celebrate Ukrainian Christmas properly. Accordingly, I tried to "organize" (camp slang for stealing) some vegetables so that we could make borscht, the traditional Ukrainian beet soup.

I actually managed to scrounge a few beets and potatoes. We had all the basic ingredients we needed. My friend Petro Mirchuk, number 49734, was another one of the *Banderivtsi* at Auschwitz. He was popular with the other inmates, especially some of the younger Jews, who often referred affectionately to him as Father. He had worked as a lawyer and knew Yiddish well, and so he had an understanding and sympathy for the Jews in Auschwitz. He was then running the boiler in the laundry. I got to know him there, and we helped each other when we could. So, when I got these precious potatoes and beets, I passed them to him so that he could cook them in the steam.

As I was carrying the soup that Petro had steamed to Block 17, I was stopped by an assistant roll-call leader by the name of Kaduck. He was a real sadist. As far as I knew, his only skill in life was knowing how to murder people. He saw that I was carrying a pail, and he ran over to take it away. At that moment one of the Germans, a report *führer* (leader) by the name of Hartswing, saw us. He yelled at Kaduck to halt and came over to investigate what was happening. I told him that I was a member of the *Bandera* movement, as the Nazis called Ukrainian nationalists, and explained that we celebrated Christmas on 7 January, according to the Julian calendar. I said that I had found the ingredients for soup in the garbage outside the kitchen and claimed that I had made it myself, without anyone's help. I said that my plan was to take it to the barracks and share it with my friends. Hartswing checked my tattoo number and asked me why I wasn't wearing a badge on my jacket. I said that I was a Ukrainian. He took out a scrap of cloth and wrote a big *U* on it. I said that if I wore such a badge I'd be identified as an *Ungar*, or Hungarian, and so he took it back and changed it to *Ur* for *Ukrainian*. I think that badge was unique. Then he let me go. I am quite sure that, if he hadn't intervened, Kaduck would have killed me right then and there, claiming that I was a thief.

We were marched out of Auschwitz on the Feast of Jordan, 19 January 1945. I had fallen quite ill by that time and was so weak that I couldn't really walk. If it had not been for two of my friends, Yaroslav Pavlyshyn and Roman Kostiuk (who survived the war, only to die in 1952 on an OUN mission to Ukraine), I would have died. They half-carried and half-dragged me with them. We left at night. The rumors were that the Red Army was already at Cracow. So, between 10:00 and 11:00 that evening, we were told to get ready to go, and at about 1:00 a.m. we were paraded and counted up. I walked through the *Arbeit Macht Frei* gate one last time. I was free of Auschwitz, but gave it no thought. I was almost a *musulman*.

The night was cold and snowy. We were stretched out in a long column, five prisoners abreast. We were marched to a large barn, and from there we were loaded onto a train of open railway cars with no protection against the elements. We were transported to Mauthausen, in Austria, where we arrived in the afternoon of 21 January.

Mauthausen, at first impression, was even worse than Auschwitz. It was very cold, and huge numbers of people were forced into a very small space between two barbed-wire fences. So many people were pushed into that cordoned area that, if you fell, you would be trampled to death. They just let us stand there, for hours, until the early evening. Then they moved us into a shower room where we were sprayed with hot water and disinfectants. There were not enough clothes to go around. We were naked and we were forced back out into the night. Finally we were taken into a cold barracks, assigned bunks, and left for four days. Most of us were stark naked.

It was a freezing-cold January. I was on a bunk with Petro Mirchuk and Danylo Chaikivskyi, number 57373. We huddled together on the bare boards and rotated positions so that everyone had a chance to warm up. The man in the middle was the warmest. Once he had revived, he would move to the outer position, closest to the window, and the man who had been nearest the window would take his place. Our body heat was all we had to keep us from freezing to death.

Finally, they came and began sorting us out. I got a new number at Mauthausen, number 120169, although this one was not tattooed on my body. We got clothes to wear. Some of the Ukrainians, like Mirchuk, were sent to another concentration camp near Melk. It was part of the Mauthausen complex, but the prisoners there were a little better off. I was not lucky enough to be sent to Melk. Instead, I was transported again.

On 29 January 1945, I become part of a slave-labor group at the sub-camp at Ebensee. I remained in that part of Austria until the end of the war.

Ebensee was a killing field. There were enormous stone quarries there, and we labored building great tunnel complexes that were to be used to manufacture V-2 rockets. It was back-breaking work performed by men who had little food and inadequate tools. We had to march more than a kilometer, over very rough terrain, just to get to the main work sites. It was very frightening, murderous. We worked twelve hours a day. The tunnels were damp. Sometimes water would punch through and soak us, or huge stones would calve off the rock face and crush the limbs or heads of those working below. We could do little for the seriously injured because there was no doctor or medicine. The guards finished off those who were unable to work. As we marched to and from work, the SS guards would beat anyone who fell out of line or faltered. Sometimes they would beat them to death.

Many Italians perished there, as did many Soviet Ukrainians. I also saw some of the Jews who had worked in the *sonderkommando* in Auschwitz at Ebensee.

The *sonderkommando* had performed such tasks as removing gold teeth and other valuables and transporting corpses. These Jews survived the war, but I do not know where they went after that. I have never heard of any of them being punished for their crimes.

I avoided the backbreaking work as much as I could, although the penalty for shirking was death. I was caught once by the block senior. He demanded to know why I was not at work. I explained that I was cleaning our barracks. He threw me to the ground and beat me so badly that I couldn't get up. I had to crawl on all fours to get to my bunk. Then the block supervisor came by. Seeing me in my bunk, he began to beat me even harder than the block senior had. I would have died, then and there, if my tormentor had not been called away. I lay in a daze on the floor for half an hour before my vision cleared. I managed to crawl under the bunk and tuck myself out of sight. I wanted to sleep, but I knew that if I missed roll call that evening I'd be hunted down and killed. I lay there shivering and bleeding, little more than a cowering animal, until my friends came back from work. "He's ash by now," someone said when they saw that I was not in my bunk. They concluded that I had been killed. I heard them. I moved and got my head out from under the bunk. That was as far as I could crawl with what remained of my strength. My friend Vasyl Lesiuk saw me.

"Get up," he said. "Roll call is about to be sounded. If you don't show up for roll call, they'll kill you."

"Let them kill me."

I had given up. I did not even try to get up. The fellows pulled me from under the bunk and tried to stand me on my feet. I couldn't manage. They took me under the arms and hauled me out with them to the *appellplatz* (courtyard). These roll calls often took up to two hours, and that night it was raining. Everyone was soaked, and I could not stand. Sitting was forbidden. In despair, I searched for a place to rest. Spotting a bench near the chief supervisor's block, I asked my friends to take me there. They refused. I persisted until they said that they would let me go if I could walk to the bench myself. I tried. I fell flat on my face in the mud. They quickly lifted me up and held me up until roll call was over. They got me back to our barracks and into my bunk.

The barracks boss came by the next morning. I had not had my hair cut, and the cross pattern in my hair caught his attention. Inmates were supposed to have their hair cut very short. We wanted to keep it as long as possible because it provided some warmth. Once our hair got too long, the guards would cut a cross pattern on our heads as a sign that we should get it cut. When he saw that I had not been shaved, he began to beat me. I protested that I had been too ill to go. He asked what was wrong with me. I replied I had an acute case of diarrhea. My friends intervened at that point. They told him that I was sick, and they asked him to leave me alone. Surprisingly, he did.

I did many different jobs while I was with the slave-labor group at Ebensee. For about a week I worked with the team that kept the surrounding roads clear of snow and carried railway ties. It was hard work because of the damp and the cold. I was even more miserable because my boots had fallen apart. I was working with no footwear. When I reported to my supervisor, respectfully begging (as we were obliged to) for a new pair of boots, he began yelling at me, insisting that I had deliberately lost my pair. I denied losing my boots and was given a new pair in the morning. But they were soaking wet. I had to go out into the cold and work all day in wet boots.

I lasted two days in wet boots. My feet were so swollen that I asked for permission to see the camp medic. This enraged the supervisor. He screamed that he was sick and tired of malingerers like me who didn't want to work. We were marched out for work, but when the call went out, "Work teams, form into groups!" I stood aside and joined the group of those going for a medical exam. The doctor had a list of the numbers of the prisoners who were permitted to see him. Mine was not one of them. I was reported. They forced me to go to work that day. By the next day my inability to walk was so obvious that I was finally given permission to see the medic.

At Ebensee, conditions were rough for everyone. Even the SS men who guarded us did not have enough food—not that we cared if they were suffering. We ate a kind of soup made of weeds and potato peels, sometimes with tree bark mixed in. We'd cook anything that was even remotely edible. Men who were expected to work long, hard hours digging tunnels and quarrying rock could not survive on it. My friends started to die off.

Volodymyr Klymko, my lawyer friend who had studied in Prague, died right in front of my eyes. We were stumbling along the path to the quarry for another day's work. One moment he was shuffling along; the next he was near my feet, dead. We had to drag his body back to the camp so that it could be counted.

The figures, you must remember, had to add up.

They dumped his body into the crematorium, and he was gone. Off the roll call, off the earth. Danylo Chaikivskyi, a journalist, tried to encourage us by saying that the war would soon end and that we must not give up hope.

We suspected that the war was coming to an end. What would happen to us? That became a nagging question. Would the Nazis exterminate us and bury our bodies? Would they try to hide the evidence of their mass murders and their slave-labor camps? Added to our deteriorating physical condition, this psychological strain further debilitated us. We worried constantly.

We tried to maintain our solidarity. I will always remember how we Ukrainians came together for Latin Easter, toward the end of March 1945. We had been given the day off. It was the last time that the ten or so of us who still survived in Ebensee would be together—at least on this earth. We spent Easter together, trying to give each other a little hope, telling each other that the war would soon be over, that if we endured just a little longer we would survive. Most of my comrades did not.

One day, as I was walking back from the quarry, a *kapo* yelled at me, saying that I was not moving fast enough. He hit me, forcing me to the ground. I barely managed to get up. I had given up. The next day I went to the camp medic. He could see the state that I was in and so put me off work for a few days. I knew that I could no longer take the heavy work in the quarries or tunnels. I said so. I was assigned to cleanup duties around the camp, aided by another Ukrainian, Volodia, from the region of Volhynia. At this stage in the war there was virtually nothing left for any of us to eat. Supplies were not getting through; the Third Reich was collapsing. We ate coal. We ate more tree bark, anything to fill our bellies, anything that might give us at least the illusion of having something to eat. We were dying on our feet.

My diarrhea became acute. No one bothered to treat me. It was just a matter of time before I died. They took me and laid me in a room adjacent to the ovens of the crematorium. That way they wouldn't have to carry my corpse so far. I lay on tar paper, on a dirty concrete floor. I was fouled by my own excrement, pus, and blood. My sores became badly infected, and parts of my buttocks were bruised due to lack of circulation. I have dark spots on my body to this day that remind me of those festering wounds.

As I lay there waiting to die, they brought in my friends,

one by one. Nykyfor Tatsii came to lie beside me, then Volodia Savchuk. Nykyfor died first. He went right into the oven. We could see them burn him. Then Vasyl died, and his body went into the same oven. Finally, only Volodia and I were left. We had no clothes at all. We huddled together, trying to stay warm and alive. I knew Volodia had died when the warmth of life went out of him. I pushed myself away from him. The last of my Ukrainian comrades from Auschwitz went into the crematorium at Ebensee.

A Pole who had been assigned to be a medic came by. He discovered that I was still alive. He had been one of those magnificently defiant heroes who had dared to fight the Nazis in the Warsaw uprising. He asked me, in Polish, where I was from. For no reason that I have ever been able to explain, I replied, in Polish, that I was from the city of Tarnów and had lived on Sanguszka Street. I'd never been there, but I just blurted these details out. He was stunned. He too had lived in Tarnów. He had lived on Sanguszka Street when he had been attending medical school. Thankfully he didn't ask me for a street number. He told me not to drink the lime concoction we had been given. He said that it was intended only to speed us on to our Maker. He gave me some pills to swallow, and later he came back and helped move me to a barracks room. He placed me in a lower bunk and gave me a blanket. He told the barracks senior not to bother me—I was very sick and under his personal care. Despite his kindness, I was so ill that I don't recall much of what happened. I remember that I was moved again and left unmolested. I also remember that he said he was from Piotrków. I am still looking for him so that I can thank him for saving my life. I lapsed into semi-consciousness. I was dying. It was late April 1945.

For those who survived Ebensee, the war ended on 8 May 1945. The Americans arrived. I don't remember the day. Somehow, and I have no recollection of how, I had been taken for dead. A few days before I had been thrown onto a pile of corpses awaiting cremation. That is where I lay, in the cold embrace of the dead. They were men like me, who had been brought to this place and worked to death. They were men whom I had never had the opportunity to meet in this world. I lay there outside the oven.

I would have been shoved into the oven that had already consumed so many others if it had not been for my OUN comrades from the Melk camp. On Ukrainian Easter, 6 May 1945, Hryhorii Naniak and Oleksa Vintoniak had come over to the Ebensee enclosure to look for me and other survivors. They had just about given up and were leaving when they saw me twitching on a pile of corpses. I was atop my own Golgotha (the common name for the spot where Christ was crucified), near the crematorium building, ready to be burned alive. They pulled me down from the pile and saved me from those flames. I came back to the world of the living on the very day that Ukrainians celebrate the Resurrection of Christ.

The next few days are not clear in my mind. The Americans liberated us. I know that I slept for hours after we were taken out of Ebensee. I was moved to a nearby field where American army medics and German nurses stripped us naked and washed and deloused us. Our wounds were treated, and we were given blankets and left to sleep.

The war in Europe ended on 8 May 1945, VE Day. I knew nothing of this. I remained in a half-conscious world for nearly three weeks. My recovery was very gradual. Many who should have died earlier, died now. They had held on long enough to see the death of Nazi Germany. Now, even though they no longer had to work and were getting better rations and medical attention, they could die with some semblance of peace. They knew, at the last, that they had vanquished their tormentors.

Babyn Yar

SONJA DUNN

In September 1941, the Nazis occupied Kyiv, the capital of Ukraine, and ordered all of the Jews to gather with their suitcases and valuables, tricking them into thinking they were being transported to safety. Instead, they were marched to Babyn Yar (which means "grandmother's ravine") and shot. More than 30,000 Jews were killed in 36 hours. More than 100,000 people were executed there, including Ukrainians, Russians, Poles, and Gypsies.

Babyn Yar
Babyn Yar
Babyn Yar
to celebrate the slaughter
the drums beat
the tanks roar
the aircraft circle
to mask deafening reports
from Nazi soldiers' guns
"We are drunk
we stagger
we are wild
we become inhuman

we cannot hear
we cannot really see
these unclothed bodies
of the maimed
of the women
of the children
of Gypsies Jews Ukrainians
falling
falling
falling
into Babyn Yar"

A Canadian writer
I stand on Babyn Yar

It is said that beneath us
we can find brains
babies' shoes
nannies' embroidered blouses
under us lie
the ravaged

Nakedness made them invisible

1945

A Bar of Chocolate

NATALIA BUCHOK

World War II spawned thousands of refugees. They were called "displaced persons," or DPs. My father was one of them. In the fall of 1944, as the Germans retreated and the Soviets moved back in, he escaped from his home village in the Carpathian Mountains of Ukraine. He was a seventeen-year-old boy who had already survived the German occupation when so many had not. His mother, fearing for his safety under the repressive regime of the Soviets, sent him away. He walked across Europe, eventually ending his journey in a DP camp (refugee camp) in Germany, where he ran into his father, who had fled some time before him. My father believes that the DP camp he stayed in had previously been a forced-labor camp. He has often repeated this story to me. It is one that I first listened to with great astonishment. The names of the people involved have been changed.

Katrusia strolled by a group of American soldiers bartering their rations to a bevy of blonde German girls for haircuts, laundry services, and other things. The sight of the ration containers—filled with cans of meat, cigarettes, sugar, coffee, soap, gum, and chocolate—sent the girls into a swooning frenzy.

117

Katrusia's mouth watered at the sight of the silver foil packages. Her fingers itched to reach out, grab a chunk of chocolate, and shove it into her mouth. She imagined its solid texture dissolving on her tongue and filling her mouth with its dark and velvet sweetness. Chocolate. Such a luxury. She couldn't imagine trading it away.

The soldiers had a way they carried themselves—a cocky confidence that she hadn't seen in a long time. There were times over the past three years when she had been so afraid that now she felt drawn to their strength, like the tide to the moon, helpless to resist its magnetic pull. The war had taught her what a coward she was. She had groveled for kind words, bartered her body to stay alive, and done far worse than flirt in order to eat.

Katrusia caught the eye of one of the soldiers and sidled closer. He broke through the group with an eager, welcoming smile. Lowering her eyes, she smiled demurely and swung her skirt, answering his smile with a calculated shyness.

Within several minutes, she'd managed to finagle a chocolate and some sugar out of the soldier, as well as some cigarettes. His name was Peter, and because he made her feel safe and special, she agreed to meet him later that evening. Peter and his brethren had to return to their duties, and she had to return to camp.

She hated going back there. It reminded her too much of her life as an *osterbeiter* (slave laborer—literally, "eastern worker"). She didn't sleep well in the DP barracks, where the unhappy, crowded conditions fueled nightmares and restless sleep. She preferred to stay away as much as possible.

She continued to dawdle, turning off the main road and following a path that bordered a farmer's field.

Perched on a familiar boulder, underneath a tree green with buds, she hunched her shoulders against the cool breeze. From this far away, she could just barely imagine that the whispers of smoke purling into the air came from the houses of neighbors,

Natalia's father, Michael Buchok.

friends, and family, though the town in the distance was nothing like the village where she had grown up.

"Katya."

She glanced around, startled, then smiled. "Misha."

She liked being with Mykhailo. She didn't have to flirt; she didn't have to wonder what he wanted from her, or to pretend. She could just be herself. Being with him was…restful.

"I didn't see you at lunch. I've been looking for you all day."

She shrugged. "I was in town."

He squatted at her feet, stroking the brittle winter grass. "Did you see the American soldiers?"

She nodded, a slight smile curving her lips. "I did more than see them."

"Katya," he said, giving her arm a shake, "what are you saying?"

"Oh, nothing," she said nonchalantly, fingering her dress. "Just that I met one of the soldiers, Peter. We have a date later tonight. I hope he's going to give me some stockings."

"A date?" he asked. "With an American soldier?"

"Yes. Why not?" she sniffed. "Don't you think I'm good enough?"

"Of course I do! In fact, I think you're too good to—"

"To what?" she asked with a bitter little smile.

"I didn't mean it like that, and you know it." He shrugged. "If you want to go on a date with him, then by all means do so. Just—be careful." Mykhailo frowned at her, his hazel eyes full of concern.

"Who knows? Maybe he'll fall in love with me, and marry me, and take me to America." Katrusia giggled at the thought.

"Katya, be realistic. He probably just wants a bit of fun."

"Well, I want a bit of fun, too—what's wrong with that?"

"Why are you suddenly so set on marrying an American, anyway? It's all you talk about lately." He stared at her, perplexed.

She leaned in close to him, poking a finger in his chest. "Because he can take me away from all this." She waved a hand in the direction of the camp.

He plucked a blade of grass and began tearing it into tiny pieces. "You don't have to get married just to get away from here."

She stared at him resentfully. "Oh, really? Well, I don't have wings or a magic carpet. Maybe it's different for you—you're a man. Or at least you will be soon," she amended as she took in his scrawny form and unshaven cheeks. "What can I do but marry? And whom should I marry? Ivan Ksenych? Please! Besides, I'm sick of this place, sick of war, sick of being hungry and having to beg for help. I want to wear nice dresses," she smoothed a hand over her worn frock, "and to eat good food, and to dance—and, oh, just to have fun and laugh again!"

She didn't mention returning home because it was an impossibility. Mykhailo knew, as did she, that returning to a village that was once again under Soviet control would be a move straight onto a cattle car headed for Siberia and its dreaded concentration camps. She would be branded a traitor for having worked in a German munitions factory. The Soviets, already awash in blood, wouldn't care that she had been a slave laborer. She had no intention of shedding one more drop of blood for them, especially when it was her own.

Mykhailo shrugged. "I think you're wasting your abilities. Why don't you get involved in some of the camp activities? Marusia is organizing a theatre group—"

"Marusia!" Katrusia scoffed. "She'd never let me participate."

"I could put in a good word for you."

Katrusia didn't respond for a moment. "I don't read very well."

"So what? There's lots being organized, and lots of things you could do—help with the children, learn how to read better, or go to school—make something of yourself. Me—I'm planning on going to school in Munchen."

She laughed. "Oh, Misha! I'm not from a big city like Lviv, or well educated like Marusia or some of the others. My family, my village—we were poor and I...I just, I don't know. I never thought about it, I guess, but I hoped that I would get married and have children." She rested her chin on her palm, sighing. "But then the Soviets came; later, the Germans. This horrible war changed everything. I just want things to be the way they used to be."

Mykhailo scattered the bits of grass about him. "They'll never be the way they used to be."

"I know," she said glumly.

"Here." Mykhailo pulled out a bundle of green fabric and handed it to her. "I got you something."

"What is it?" She fingered it in wonderment, then shook it out. Her jaw dropped. "A jacket! Where did you get this?"

He hunched one shoulder. "Oh, you know me."

She grinned and laughed again, clasping the jacket to her breast. "Yes, I do know you! How wonderful—thank you so much!" She leaned down and hugged him, then straightened up and held out the jacket again, examining its stitching and the warm lining. Trying the jacket on, she snuggled into its warmth and shut her eyes in pleasure.

Mykhailo grabbed her hand. "Come on. Let's get back to camp. They're going to serve dinner soon, and I'm starving."

"Misha."

"What?"

She stared at their joined hands, worrying her lip with her teeth. She slid him a look, then turned away, blushing.

"What is it?" He asked her, puzzled.

"I...the jacket—I don't have anything to give you for it."

"I know that!" Mykhailo scoffed.

"No," she whispered, "you don't understand." She felt her face flush. Refusing to look at him, she stammered, "I c-could, you know...do it with you if you want."

"Katrusia!" He was speechless for a moment. "I would never ask that of you; you know that."

Her face burned hotter. "I know. I know you wouldn't ask— but I'm offering."

He pulled his hand out of hers, his face red with indignation and embarrassment. "Katya—I can't. I wouldn't. And you—you shouldn't be doing this."

"It's the only thing I have to offer," she explained angrily, furious with herself for even suggesting that he would want, or accept, payment from her.

"Katya..." He hesitated, then continued gently, "You don't have to offer me anything."

For the first time in a long time, she felt shame. Offering payment had never seemed so wrong, not when she traded her favors for food at the factory, or when she traded them in order to be taken into a shelter during an air raid. It had been so long since someone had been kind, just for the sake of being kind, that her eyes stung with tears and her throat hurt. "I'm sorry," she choked out. "I wasn't thinking. It's just that, sometimes—"

"Stop." He cut her off. "You don't have to explain to me." He gave her arm a shake. "I'm your friend, for God's sake. Don't ever—" He let out an explosive sigh. "Look, let's just forget about it—and in the future, if you need anything, come to me. I'll get it for you."

She began weeping in earnest.

"What are you crying for?" Mykhailo asked, exasperated.

"I don't know," she sobbed.

"Well, then, why do it? It doesn't help, does it? Anyway, there's nothing to cry about," he added.

She smiled at him through her tears, then laughed, hiccupping. "Oh, Misha! If I can ever do you a good turn, I will. You're a true friend."

They began walking, arm in arm. She heard foil rustle in her skirt pocket. She stopped, pulling her arm from his. "Wait! I just remembered."

"What?"

She dug through her pocket and retrieved a silver foil package, holding it up with a triumphant cry. "I have something for you after all. Chocolate!"

"Chocolate?" Mykhailo's eyes grew round. "I've never had chocolate."

"Ooh, you'll love it, then. Go ahead, try it," she added, as he hesitated, turning the package over and over in his hands.

He slowly unwrapped it, then lifted the squares of chocolate up to his nose, sniffing. "It smells good."

"Wait until you taste it."

Someone came running into the barracks, the wooden boards clattering under pounding feet, the sound reverberating through the building like an alarm. For a moment it drowned out the sound of the rain thrumming against the roof.

Mykhailo stared unseeing at the pictures pinned above his bed and chewed his lip, his mind a few hundred kilometers away. His father Vasyl sat on Ivan's bunk, mending a shirt, as careful and patient with it as he would have been with one of his horses.

Ivan stood in the doorway smoking a cigarette. "Hey, Mykhailo. How about paying attention when someone talks to you?"

"Maybe if you had something worth saying, he'd listen better," Vasyl said without looking up from his mending.

Ivan ignored him, turning his shoulder to the wall. "What are you thinking about so seriously?" he asked, blowing out rings of smoke.

Mykhailo rolled over on his side and propped himself up on an elbow. "About what that guy from the *Ukrainsky Dopomohey Komitet* (Ukrainian Relief Committee) said yesterday—that they'll be offering free schooling in Munchen."

His father snorted. "School—is that all you ever think about? You should think about finding work."

"I thought you wanted me to get an education. You were the one who wanted me to be a priest."

His father frowned, blinking hard, and his voice shook. "That was before the war, when I had a son to give to the priesthood."

Ivan piped up. "School is good. He could become a teacher, and then, when we all go back to our villages—"

"Another fool. You think we can ever go back? The Soviets will kill us," Vasyl interrupted Ivan, glancing around uneasily.

"The Americans will make sure that doesn't happen," Ivan insisted.

Petro Zelenych's eyes narrowed on the piece of wood that he was whittling. "The Americans aren't going to go fight the Soviets; they're allies. They didn't want to enter the war in the first place, and they've promised not to interfere with repatriation attempts by the Soviets,"

"That can't be true—I don't believe it," Ivan said, thrusting his jaw out.

"I've always said you were a fool, Ivan Ksenych, and here's my proof," Vasyl said with disgust.

"What? What did I say?"

"I've heard that the Soviets have already started forcibly repatriating, with the Americans looking the other way. You know what that means, don't you?" Petro asked the group at large, his hands spouting shavings that fell in crisp, curling heaps onto his pants and the floor around him.

They exchanged glances, dark with knowledge. They would be branded as traitors. Torture and death would await those who went home. Under those circumstances, there were few who were eager to return.

Ivan's face fell. "Maybe you're right. But even if you are, being a teacher is a good thing, no matter where you are living. It'll get him a good job eventually, *Paneh* (Mister) Buchok," Ivan said, returning to the original subject, like a dog following a scent.

Mykhailo's father shrugged. "Maybe." He stared at the ground, his face gloomy. "But in the meantime, we need to eat."

Ivan waved expansively at the room. "We're eating, aren't we?"

"That's here. Who knows what it'll be like in Munchen?"

"No, but..."

Mykhailo let Ivan keep arguing. Poor Ivan didn't know there wasn't any point to it.

Ivan yelped, jumping up, and slapped at his leg. "Those damn *blushtitsi* (bedbugs)!" He glared at Mykhailo resentfully. "How can you bear to lie around?"

Mykhailo shifted on the straw mattress, listening to it rustle, as a bedbug scuttled out. He smacked it sharply with the flat of his hand, then flicked away the dead bug. "The *blushtitsi* don't bother me the way they bother you."

Ivan shook his head in disbelief. "It's amazing. God must've really blessed you."

Vasyl stood up, shaking out the shirt. "God blessed you too, Ivan Ksenych. Not with brains or wisdom. But, hey, you're still alive, aren't you?" He strode out of the room, his footfalls sure and even on the wooden floors.

Ivan scratched his head. "I think he's still mad at me."

Mykhailo smiled wryly. "It's not just that. You should know. He's always in a bad mood."

"Because of the war?" Petro asked sympathetically.

Mykhailo sat up, smoothing his rumpled bedding. "That's part of it."

Petro and Ivan exchanged glances.

"What's the other part?" Petro asked.

Mykhailo shrugged. "It was the NKVD (People's Commissariat for Internal Affairs, later known as the KGB, or the Secret Police)."

Ivan sank down onto his bed. "The NKVD? *Bozhe milostyvi* (Merciful God)!" He crossed himself hurriedly, the smoke from his cigarette temporarily obscuring his features.

Petro stopped his whittling, and the room was silent but for the sound of the rain. "What happened?" he asked in a hushed voice.

Mykhailo shrugged again. "The usual. They came in the middle of the night and took him away for three days." He paused, staring blindly at the wall. "When he came back, he was a different person."

"What did they do to him?" Ivan asked with a sort of morbid curiosity, as if knowing the details might better prepare him to face them, should he ever have to do so.

"I never found out. I know that they wanted him to betray his neighbors by denouncing them as traitors. In the end, he ran away. You can imagine. He was terrified of what the NKVD would do to him." Mykhailo stared at his hands. He wished he had something to whittle, some soft piece of wood that he could dig a knife into and shave pieces from, the way the Germans and the Soviets had whittled his life away, bit by bit. "He never spoke about it, but he started being afraid all the time, and he hasn't stopped since."

"And his family?" Petro asked softly.

Mykhailo picked at a thread hanging from his trousers. "He left us behind."

"My God, no!" Ivan gasped.

Mykhailo shrugged. "My God, yes."

"They—" Ivan swallowed hard. "What did they do to your family?"

"You're stinking up the place with your cigarette." The barracks chairman's grating voice broke over them.

Ivan turned with a sardonic lift of his lip. "Oh. And how is that worse than the stink of the place when I'm not smoking?"

The chairman scowled in response, then turned to Mykhailo. "Hey, Buchok, Katrusia's looking for you."

Mykhailo jumped up. Anything to break the tedium of camp life, especially when it rained. And anything to avoid revisiting memories that were better left in the past. He left Ivan and Petro gaping at him, their unanswered question lingering in the air between them.

He jogged over to Katrusia's barrack, hunching his shoulders against the cold spring downpour. There were times when he understood his father and the paralyzing fear that ruled him. Then there were times when Mykhailo didn't understand his father at all, especially the abandonment they'd all suffered at his hands.

He paused at the door to Katrusia's barrack and shook the worst of the rain from his clothes. Everything was gray: the day, the rain, the wooden barracks, even the mud looked gray. He sighed. Whatever it was that the NKVD had done to his father, they'd scarred his soul, and there was nothing he, or anyone else, could ever do to change him back again.

Katrusia leaned over Marusia's bed, her hair clinging in cold, damp strands to her cheeks. She dangled a pair of silk stockings in Marusia's frowning face. "See what I got?" She shoved them back into her dress pocket with a smug smile. She spared an envious glance for the boards above Marusia's bunk, where a few faded photographs of Marusia's brother and sisters hung, their faces stiff and uncomfortable as they posed for the camera in their embroidered finery. Her own sleeping area was devoid of any such mementos.

Marusia sniffed her disapproval and rustled the papers that she held. "I could say what I think of someone who goes with a soldier in return for payment, but I won't."

"Tell me I didn't just run over here to listen to you girls argue." Mykhailo stood in the doorway, his clothes streaked from the rain, his blonde hair curling and dripping. He looked so young, until you looked into his eyes, and then he looked so old. It was an odd contrast.

"Oh, just ignore her, Misha! She's a sourpuss because no one ever asks her out," Katrusia said as she flounced over to him, uncomfortable with her own thoughts.

Marusia sat up with an indignant scowl. "I get asked all the time—I just have better sense than to run with every soldier who asks me. You—you have more *dates* than sense, and one of these days it'll get you in trouble."

"Marusia, Katya—stop it. You're getting on my nerves," Mykhailo said, wiping his face with a corner of his shirt. He leaned against the wall, water dripping from his clothes and forming a puddle under him, a puddle that intensified the smell of the barracks, the damp, stifling smell of mold, rot, and rain.

"I'm sorry, Misha," Katrusia said with a shamefaced look at him as she reached for a blanket. She took it to him and threw it around his shoulders. "Misha, you have to do me a favor," she said, tucking the blanket close about his neck.

"What?"

She glanced at him, wondering if he'd disapprove. "I have a date tonight with Peter, that American soldier I told you about, remember?"

"So, he's come sniffing around again, the one who promised to take you to New York?" Marusia asked sarcastically as she bent over her papers. "Or, no, wasn't that Danny? Or maybe John? Sam? Tony?"

Katrusia glared at her. "Well, this one means it."

"Marusia," Mykhailo said, injecting a note of warning into his voice, "if you don't stop baiting Katya, I—"

Marusia jumped to her feet. "Oh, all right, already!" She stomped down the barrack, pounding on the wooden boards for emphasis so they clattered as loudly as the *kalatalo* (a wooden instrument that makes a loud, clacking sound) at church on Good Friday.

Mykhailo walked over and threw himself across Katrusia's bunk.

She perched on the edge of the cot, her head canted to one side. "Well, Peter has a friend who also needs a date for tonight. I told him I'd bring a girl along."

Mykhailo stared at her, baffled. "So? What does that have to do with me?"

She rolled her eyes. "Well, I've asked Hania, and I've asked Irka. Neither of them want to go with me—they say those *chlopchistvo* (guys) they're dating would pitch a fit. And then I had the brilliant idea of taking you along."

Mykhailo gawked at her. "Me? In case you haven't looked closely enough, I'm no girl."

She gave a lighthearted laugh. "I know that, silly! But you're very handsome—almost pretty." She leaned back, narrowing her eyes in calculation, and studied his lanky form. "And I think, with the right clothes and some makeup, you could pass for a girl."

He turned over on his side and shut his eyes. "Of all the stupid—! Forget it—I'm not dressing up as a girl."

"Ahhh, but I didn't tell you the best part. You'll get some chocolate if you come along."

He cracked open an eye. "Chocolate?"

"Yes, chocolate. The American soldier will give you chocolate."

He frowned at her, as he thought over her proposition. "Would I have to wear a dress?"

"Well, of course! But, just think—he'll probably give you a whole bar of chocolate."

"A whole bar?"

Katrusia nodded and watched Mykhailo.

"A whole bar of chocolate," he repeated softly, speculatively. "You said you liked it."

"No," he said, slowly. "I didn't like it."

"You didn't?"

"Nooo—"

"But, I thought—"

"I loved it!"

She giggled. "Oh, Misha!"

He pushed himself up onto his elbows. "When?"

"This evening." She sat back, satisfied.

He fingered his chin doubtfully. "Do you really think I could pass as a girl?"

"Sure. Why not?"

He put a hand to his short, masculine haircut. "Well, my hair, for one."

She flapped a hand at him in dismissal. "No problem. We put a nice scarf on your head, and you have those wavy bangs— no one will know the difference. Just don't take that scarf off." She leaned forward and stroked her hand along his chin. "Thank goodness you don't shave yet—that would've been a lot more difficult to hide. Right now your skin is as soft as a girl's."

He jerked his chin away in embarrassment.

Katya laughed softly. "Oh, Misha, thank God for your lack of a beard. Tonight it will bring you chocolate."

They left the DP barracks with Mykhailo stumbling after Katrusia, trying to walk in the high-heeled pumps. "How do you girls manage on these?" he gasped, wobbling.

She smiled over her shoulder and wiggled her hips as she pranced along. "Practice, just practice."

"More like torture," he muttered. He wondered if the NKVD or the Gestapo had ever thought of using women's shoes to torture men. He thought it would've been effective. He was ready to do anything, just to be able to take them off.

He stopped and said, "That's it. I'm walking barefoot until we get there, and then I'll put them on."

Katrusia rushed back to him. "No, no, that might be a mistake. If your feet swell up, you won't be able to get the shoes back on. Better to leave them on. You can take them off on your way back. Oh, and by the way, don't wait for me, okay?" She winked at him.

He put his hands on his knees and let his head drop, then straightened with a grimace. "It had better be good chocolate."

They left the DP barracks behind and began the trek to Weissenberg. The moon was full that night, lighting their way. In the distance, the lights of Weissenberg sparkled like fireflies.

He cursed those shoes a million times. He struggled to not lose his balance and fall down, tripping first over the roadway, and later, when they entered Weissenberg, over the uneven cobblestones.

The meeting place was a lone bench in the middle of a small orchard of headless trees. Once a park, perhaps, or someone's garden—it was hard to tell now. The one bomb that had fallen on Weissenberg had fallen into this hapless grove. Sitting side by side on a felled tree, he and Katrusia waited for the American soldiers to arrive.

"If he tries to kiss me, I'm going to punch him," he said, wincing as he clipped on the earrings Katrusia had lent him.

Katrusia sighed in exasperation. "Don't punch him. Just slap him, and then he'll think nothing of it."

The loud rumble of an army jeep broke the silence of the cool spring night. Katrusia ran up to greet the soldiers. Mykhailo hung back, eyeing them nervously, wondering which one would be his "date." Katrusia strolled back, hanging off the arm of a short soldier.

"This is Peter, and that's Tom." She tilted her head back at the other soldier, a large, meaty fellow. With an evil glint in her eye, she introduced Mykhailo as "Maria," short for "Marusia."

"We're taking off. Have fun." And with a swing of her skirts, she turned and flounced off with her American soldier.

Big, beefy Tom stood there grinning at Mykhailo. Mykhailo smiled weakly, while eyeing Tom's fists. They were pretty big. If Tom found out he was a guy, he'd be lucky if he got away with only a broken nose.

"Do you want to sit down?" Tom asked eagerly, his grin widening, as his eyes traveled over the curves of Mykhailo's dress (the result of a few well-placed, balled-up socks, and a borrowed brassiere), down his legs, to his feet encased in the high-heeled pumps. Mykhailo flushed, battling an urge to express masculine indignation in a way that would quash that hot look in Tom's eyes. Instead he nodded and turned to make his way to the tree. He sat down, primly arranging his skirts so his knobby knees wouldn't show.

Tom sat down next to him and immediately put his arm on the tree limb behind Mykhailo's shoulders and leaned in close, engulfing them in a cloud of eye-watering aftershave. Mykhailo shrank away. He could feel the weight of Tom's gaze as it shifted from face to mouth to throat. Mykhailo prayed that the makeup Katrusia had applied would bear up under such close scrutiny.

"You're a real looker, you know that?"

Mykhailo bit the side of his mouth, fighting an urge to laugh hysterically.

Tom frowned at him. "What's a matter? You *do* speak English, don't you?"

Mykhailo nodded, ducking his head. "Yes, a little."

Tom's face brightened. "Well, that's good." He cleared his throat, and his hand drifted down to rest on Mykhailo's shoulder. Mykhailo swallowed hard, holding himself rigid, fighting the instinct to bolt, tethered in place by his desire for chocolate.

"So, soldier, where America you from?" he asked, trying to speak softly so Tom wouldn't notice the bass notes in his voice.

But Tom wasn't interested in talking about America. He reached into his jacket, pulled out a tarnished silver flask, and took a long swig. He turned his face, and Mykhailo sprang to his feet, rubbing hard at his neck.

Tom frowned at him. "What's the problem, Maria?"

Mykhailo pulled surreptitiously at the dress, which felt like it was sticking to his back. He could've sworn Tom was about to nuzzle his neck, and neck nuzzling was not on the agenda this evening—not even for chocolate. "Nothing. I shy."

Tom chuckled. "Well, if that's all, that's fine by me. Just not too shy, I hope."

The flow of English came too fast for Mykhailo to really understand, but he could tell that Tom wasn't mad. He resisted an urge to wipe his face, where he felt sweat trickling along his temple. "Chocolate—you have chocolate?"

"Oh, yeah, right." Tom reached into his jacket and pulled out a rectangle of shiny silver paper. "Here it is."

Mykhailo snatched it from him and held it up to his nose. The sweet, heavy smell of chocolate wafted through the paper. "Mmm, good."

Tom grinned. "Tastes good, too. Now, why don't you come right back here and sit down." He patted the tree bench and looked at Mykhailo as if he were a piece of yummy chocolate.

Mykhailo sat down again with the greatest reluctance, muscles twitching with the urge to get far, far away from that gleam in Tom's eyes.

Tom reached into his pocket for the flask again, but this time when he pulled it out, something fell from his pocket and fluttered to the ground.

Mykhailo bent down to pick up the gleaming square of white paper.

Tom tried to grab it from him, but Mykhailo held it out of his grasp, peering at the piece of paper. It was a photograph, but it was too dark for him to make out more than that it was a photo of a woman. "Who that?"

"Never mind."

Tom wasn't leering anymore. He looked wistful and curiously vulnerable, all the brashness suddenly wiped from his face.

Mykhailo gave the picture back to Tom. "You miss." He made it a statement.

Tom looked away. "Yes."

Mykhailo fell silent. He didn't have the vocabulary to say anything more and Tom seemed lost in his own memories.

Tom lit a cigarette, the tip glowing orange against the dark night. He offered one to Mykhailo, who shook his head in refusal.

Mykhailo tucked the chocolate into his pocket. He still hadn't figured out how he was going to ditch his date.

"Aw, hell." Tom threw away his cigarette and turned to Mykhailo, one arm snaking around his shoulders, while his other hand came down hot and heavy on Mykhailo's thigh, then moved up under his dress. Mykhailo jumped like he'd had boiling water poured on his leg. He slapped Tom's hand away with enough force that he felt the shock of it up his arm.

Tom grinned, unabashed. "Sorry. Couldn't help myself getting fresh. You're just so damned pretty."

Mykhailo blinked at him, not comprehending. That had been a close call. Any higher and—

Tom got up and stretched out a hand to Mykhailo. "Let's go for a little walk."

At least Tom wouldn't be able to feel him up if they were walking. They strolled through the little park, Tom's arm around Mykhailo's shoulders. Mykhailo held himself stiffly. He eyed Tom's legs and wondered if he could outrun him. Not in these high-heels anyway. He turned his gaze to his surroundings, frantically searching the bushes and trees for a way to escape.

Tom turned, pulling Mykhailo closer. Mykhailo put his hand out on Tom's chest, balling up his other hand into a fist. Tom looked like he was getting ready to try and kiss him, and he couldn't think of another way to stop him.

But Tom didn't kiss him. "I gotta take a leak. I'll be right back. Don't you be going anywhere, now," he said with a grin.

Mykhailo watched in relief as Tom strolled to a bush and disappeared behind it.

He wasted no time. He yanked off the high heels, remembering to keep a firm grip on them, and started running. He flew down the path, then veered off it into a copse of trees, hoping that Tom would not see where he'd gone. A masculine shout made his blood run cold, and his legs pump faster. He could hear crashing in the bushes behind him, and shouts, and loud curses.

Mykhailo broke through the cover of trees and raced down a side street. He leapt over a garden fence, then scrambled through some more bushes. At least the dress made for good running. His heart pounded in his chest, drowning out the sound of his escape, and his lungs worked like a pair of bellows, the wind whistling in his ears. He bumped against a cherry tree, scraping an elbow, and his dress caught on something, pulling him up short. He yanked at it amidst a shower of pink petals and heard an ominous tearing sound. *Nai tebe kachka kopne!* (May a duck kick you!) The dress must've ripped.

"Maria!" Tom's voice came booming from somewhere behind and to the left of him.

Mykhailo freed the dress with a yank and took flight again. He ran through a yard and leapt to avoid a barely visible obstacle. The obstacle erupted in a fit of barking. Startled, Mykhailo tripped and fell against a shed, knocking some chickens from their roost. Their squawking roused the homeowner, whose shouts added to the cacophony. It didn't help when the owner got out a gun and started shooting.

Mykhailo picked up speed. *Great, just great,* he thought. Tom didn't need to be able to see Mykhailo in order to follow him—all he had to do was follow the noise.

Mykhailo ran down a side street. Back in the distance he thought he heard shots again. He wondered if the homeowner was now shooting at Tom. He sort of hoped so. Not that he wanted him hurt, but slowed down would be a good thing—a very good thing.

He continued running, weaving his way through the dark, even after he could no longer hear the sounds of pursuit.

When he finally tore into camp, his speed hadn't lessened much. He charged up to the barracks, ran in, and stumbled into his room, falling onto his cot in a heap of gasping, heaving, sweat-soaked cotton.

His breathing sounded thunderous to his ears. He was amazed he hadn't woken anyone up with his explosive run through camp. But the barracks were quiet, except for Ivan's snoring, which was good. If his father had seen what he was up to, he'd be whipped, despite being seventeen.

He eased the shoes, which he still clutched in his hand, onto the floor. Then he sat up and tore off the scarf and the earrings. He put a hand to his chest and looked down. He looked to be short a sock or two—his "breasts" were decidedly lopsided. He sighed. That had been his one good pair of socks. He then stripped as quickly as he could, contorting in order to get the bra off and undo the dress zipper. After bundling all his borrowed finery into a pile, he tied it up with the scarf and shoved it under his bed. He lay back, still breathing hard, and began laughing softly as he groped for his pants in the dark.

He froze as he remembered—he'd left them in Katrusia's room. *Damn.* What was he going to do now? He was damn well not going to put that dress on again.

Angry with himself for not having planned this better, he hid his chocolate, wrapped himself in his threadbare but scratchy blanket, and crept out of his room.

He made it to Katrusia's barrack without being seen, stopping only to wash the makeup from his face. He dropped the bundle of borrowed clothes on her bed and dressed himself quickly. If Marusia woke up and saw him, she'd probably start screaming. Luckily, she was snoring. Mykhailo grinned. Ivan should get to know her.

He had almost reached his barrack when a jeep roared into camp. A burly American soldier was hanging off the steering wheel, shouting for "my girl."

Mykhailo froze. His heart stopped for a moment, then started up again with a kick like a mule's. Tom—of course, who else could it be?—turned off his jeep and jumped out, still shouting, "My girl! Where's my girl?"

Mykhailo shrank back into the shadows, sweating and incredulous. He hadn't looked *that* pretty as a girl now, had he?

He heard the barracks chairman talking to Tom, trying to

reason with him in broken English. Tom would not be placated. Tom, it appeared, wanted "Maria."

Mykhailo watched the drama unfold, frozen in place like a rabbit under the eye of a predator. As Tom and the barracks chairman argued, a small crowd of men gathered around; so when the barracks chairman threw up his hands in exasperation and stalked off, he did so in the company of a number of men. Several others stayed back, trying to placate the increasingly irate Tom.

A feminine shriek rent the night, with more shrieks and high-pitched complaints following. The barracks chairman and his posse straggled into view, dragging behind them a group of disgruntled women, including Mrs. Popovych, who had managed to retain a pre-war chubbiness, as well as a linen shift. She looked like a snowball hurtling along the ground.

Mykhailo felt a bubble of laughter welling up inside. They had rounded up every Maria in camp! The barracks chairman, tight-lipped with anger, proceeded to parade them in their nightwear, introducing each one by pulling them forward and saying, "This Maria...and *this* Maria...and *this* Maria..."

Mykhailo put his hand over his mouth to stop himself from laughing out loud. Maria was a very popular Ukrainian name. Poor Tom stood there scratching his head, earnestly peering at each Maria. But it was no use. The Maria he wanted was not there. After a lengthy perusal (Mykhailo saw Tom recoil when he was introduced to Mrs. Popovych), he saw that it was futile. With his head hanging down and a dejected air, he climbed back into his jeep and roared off into the night. Mykhailo slumped back against the wall, in relief, and then began laughing again.

That had been a close call.

Mid–1950s

Bargain

LARRY WARWARUK

*I was born and raised in Glenavon, a village halfway
between Regina and Kenosee Lake. My childhood and
teen years took place during the booming 1950s, when I
played on the front street and worked in my parents'
general store and meat market. "Bargain" is based on
an incident from that time.*

As I stack soup cans, I hear the front door open and close.
Mrs. Kuzma stands by the entry, pulling at the fingers of her
brown cotton gloves. With her thumb and index finger, she
wipes frost from her glasses. I think she's Polish. Half of our
customers are; the other half are English. There are not many
Ukrainians in our town. Mom and Dad speak Ukrainian all the
time at home, so I will learn the language. All I know now are
the words for meal-time foods—meat, potatoes, milk.

I can't tell the difference between the Polish and the
Ukrainians. Mrs. Honchar might be Ukrainian. She is an old
woman who comes in once a week for a piece of beefsteak. I
overheard Mom tell an English neighbor lady, who had come

139

Warwaruk family store

to our house for tea, that Mrs. Honchar wore a steak as a compress on her cancerous breast.

Mrs. Kuzma glances here and there, until her gaze fixes on me. She unhooks a black string shopping bag from the crook of her arm, and, holding the bag in front of her, she slinks toward the dry-goods counter. She disappears behind the piles of flannel bedding and men's denim coveralls.

Dad told me to watch for shoplifters. He's at home having his supper. I can't imagine Mrs. Kuzma stealing—or what I'd do if I caught her. The clock strikes the half-hour. Maybe I can better watch her if I go behind the dry-goods counter to wind the clock. She's hiding in the shadows at the end of the aisle. I stand on the step stool to pull the chain on the light bulb, then I drag the stool over to the clock. Mrs. Kuzma fiddles with a stack of men's long underwear.

"Did you get a box of Christmas oranges yet this year, Mrs. Kuzma?" I wind the clock, turning the key tighter and tighter.

"Oh," she says. Her face appears from behind the folded woolen blankets. "No, I don't know yet what I'm doing at Christmas. So busy at Christmas."

I place the key in its place under the pendulum, close the glass door, and step down from the stool. The wooden boxes of oranges, tied in bundles of four, are piled at the back of the store where the drayman had left them this morning. I grab the knife that is hooked in the half-stripped banana stalk hanging from the ceiling, and I cut the straw rope that binds the boxes. I throw the pieces of rope into the fire and breathe in through my nose. I like the Christmas smell of burning coal and rope, the oiled floor, oranges, and nuts.

Mrs. Kuzma is at the nuts. She scoops her hand into a bag of walnuts and runs them through her fingers. Then she reaches into the hazelnuts, the pecans, and the filberts. Finally she reaches into the bigger sack of peanuts, which is on the floor under the front windows. Then Mrs. Kuzma wraps her black shawl about her shoulders and leaves the store.

I sit on a pop case and peel an orange. The smell of peel blends with the sugar smells of the open boxes—ribbon candy, fig bars, dried apples, raisins, shredded coconut, and dates. I look up as the front door slams.

"What the hell you sit there for?"

Mike Czernick stomps toward where I am sitting by the stove. His left leg stomps louder than his right, and his body sways at the hip with each step.

"Give me knife!" He doesn't ask; he shouts. Then he hacks bananas from the stalk. In his meaty hand, the curved blade of the knife looks like a pirate's hook.

"You by yourself?" Mike looks over to the meat counter at the back of the store. "What the hell! Your old man at home sleeping?" He tosses the peel on the floor, on the puddle of manure-stained snow that has fallen and melted from his boots. He laughs at me, shoves the banana in his mouth, and peels another. Mike has a big head covered with coarse, black hair. His thick eyebrows curve up at the ends, moving as he chews.

His lumpy ears and flared nostrils bristle with hairs. He has heavy, sausage-like lips, and a bit of mashed banana at the corners of his mouth is stained with snuff juice.

"Weigh this!" he says. He hands me the remaining bananas from the bunch he has cut from the stalk. He throws the second peel on the floor, and he stomps behind the display shelves of dried apples and raisins, to the cheese cutter. I follow, watching his hand crank the lever, turning the round of cheese.

"Your old man got lots of money," Mike says, and he chomps on his wedge of cheese.

"Don't you ever pay for anything?" I ask, making sure to keep a safe distance.

"Get me sausage! Where you keep the sausage?" He stomps away from the cheese cutter and bumps down the aisle, between the wall and the fig bars, to the back of the store, where the walk-in cooler sits behind the meat counter.

He grabs the metal handle and opens the insulated door. On the floor is a box of Christmas sausage that arrived this morning, fifty pounds of Swift-Canadian Ukrainian garlic sausage. Mike's parka drapes open. He bends over the box and handles the sausage. His arm lifts. He grips the sausage in his fingers for an instant. Two fat strands of meat dangle like exposed things, and then they vanish into the folds of his parka.

He brings out three more sausages and dumps them on the scale—four pounds, three ounces, at sixty-nine cents a pound— it comes to two dollars and ninety cents.

He has sausage inside his parka. What can I say? Can I ask if he has more? Can I ask him about the bulge in his parka? Numbers fly like magic from my mouth; numbers different from the ones on the scale.

"That's six dollars and thirty-five cents," I say, "and another forty cents for the bananas."

Mike grins. He opens his worn leather wallet and gives me

six bills and the correct change. He takes his parcels without a word and stomps out of the store.

The following Saturday he returns, this time at noon, when Mom and Dad are home for lunch. He barges in and bumps into Mrs. Kuzma, who is scooping through the Brazil nuts, and into Mrs. Honchar, who has come for her steak.

"Give me snuff!" he says, and he dumps bent nails, chaff, and change on the counter. His eyebrows twitch. A quarter rolls onto the floor and continues rolling all the way to the coal pail by the stove.

"How was the sausage?" I ask, handing him the Copenhagen.

"Good," he says. "You bet. Damn good."

Mrs. Kuzma and Mrs. Honchar peer out from behind an oak-framed display case containing boxes of black and white thread, a tray of colored spools, needles, thimbles, and hooks and eyes. Mike digs a thumbnail into the red cardboard snuff can and rips along the edge of the lid. He screws off the lid and, with thick fingers, digs into the can for snuff to place inside his bottom lip. He closes the lid, stuffs the can into his bib pocket, puts his finger to his nose, and sniffs.

My stomach knots. "So you liked the sausage." I hesitate, working up all the nerve I can. "That's good!" I say. "That's good! Because you paid double for it!"

Both ladies gasp, their eyes wide. Mike pulls away. His lips drop, and his chin stiffens. His neck turns from brown to red. His eyebrows twitch. He doesn't say a thing. He just looks away from me, and from the ladies, and limps out the door.

The ladies stare at the door. They turn to stare at me. For a minute nobody says a word.

At last Mrs. Honchar raises her hand, pointing to the meat counter at the back of the store.

"A quarter pound of beefsteak you get me," she says.

Late–1950s

Candy's Revenge

CORNELIA BILINSKY

*Walter Pankiw (Pancoe),
far right, and friends.
Aged eighteen,
taken in 1928.*

*A desire to express in some way the experience of my early
years on the farm inspired me to write "Candy's Revenge."
I recalled a specific childhood prank a visiting city cousin and
I had perpetrated, and I decided to use the incident as a focal
point around which I could capture the sights, sounds, tastes,
and smells of summer on the farm. In the late '50s, life for
me—a Ukrainian adolescent girl living on a farm—was
much different from that of my city-girl cousins. It was
certainly different from the life experienced by my own
teenage daughter in the '80s, and it was different from
the life experienced by young teenage girls today.*

144

Farm families depended heavily on their children to keep the farm going. On the outside, to my city cousins, it appeared that I was "always working" and very responsible—with many obligations to meet. Inside, I was no different from any other adolescent girl. I was often preoccupied with my appearance, self-conscious about my budding breasts, nervous and confused by attention from the opposite sex, and wanting, more than anything, just to have some fun. As a writer, I also wanted to discuss what seemed to be the culturally ingrained practice of mocking other people's idiosyncrasies. Growing up, I frequently heard my elders entertaining one another by imitating or mocking someone's speech, gait, or other quirk—usually behind their back. In part, this story is about the way that children naturally pick up on adult behavior.

"Wake up, Halia!"

Candy was sitting on top of me, pinching my nose. Her playful intrusion upon my sleep had worked better than an alarm clock. Had one of my brothers pinched my nose, I would have been mightily annoyed, but this was my cousin from Winnipeg. She had arrived just the day before, to spend the summer at our farm.

I struggled to sit up on the *pyryna* (duvet), which had been hastily turned into a bed on the living room floor the night before. Squinting into the morning sun streaming through the window, I smiled at Candy.

"I'm ready for adventure!" Candy declared as she rolled off me. "What are we doing for fun today?"

I shook my head. "Father is making hay today. I have to help Mother."

"Aw, shucks, Cuz! You're always working!"

"There's a lot to do," I explained, with an air of superiority. "That's why Dido is here. And some of the neighbors are coming to help." *Including Yurko,* I said to myself. A familiarly uncomfortable feeling suddenly overwhelmed me. Why did Father always have to ask him to help?

"Oh, well. I'm sure we'll think of something fun to do!" Leaping up, Candy dug into her suitcase. In a moment, she was dressed and ready for the day, looking pert and pretty in a white cotton blouse and navy shorts. Soft natural curls framed her face, complementing her slightly upturned nose.

I regarded my cousin with a mixture of admiration and envy. At thirteen, I was two years older than Candy. But I had never owned a pair of shorts. And my short brown hair was stubbornly straight—though in a vain effort to coax some curl into it, I had endured many a torturous night sleeping with my hair wound up into flat spirals and secured with bobby pins. Self-consciously, I reached into the cardboard box that held my wardrobe and pulled out a dress. It was a faded brown cotton print, a hand-me-down from one of my schoolmates, whose mother sewed all her dresses for her. It would have to do for today.

We bounded outdoors and headed for the summer kitchen. The small log building on the southwestern corner of our yard served us well. It was a cookhouse and dining room on hot summer days. Using the summer kitchen allowed the main house to remain cool and comfortable at night for sleeping. Mother was busy outside, plucking the feathers off a freshly killed chicken. On the ground before her were three more chickens with their heads chopped off. They clumped together in a mess of bedraggled white feathers and bloody necks, which hung limply over the edge of a milk pail.

"Oooh, Auntie. How can you do that?" Candy wrinkled up her nose.

"Creamed chicken for dinner!" I explained. "Wait till you taste it! Is everyone here already?" I inquired.

"Your boyfriend's already here! He just arrived!" Carl's voice teased me from the doorway.

"He's not my boyfriend!" I glared at my younger brother.

"Well, *Yindik* is here!" Carl reported loudly.

"Carl!" Mother scolded. "That's not nice!"

Candy was alive with interest. "Who's your boyfriend? Who's Yindik?"

"He's talking about Yurko, one of the men who are here to help today. And he's not my boyfriend!" I insisted.

Yurko was a neighbor who lived on an old homestead at the base of the Blue Hills, just beyond a large stretch of poplar woods, west of our farm. The youngest of nine siblings, the rest of whom had long since left the homestead, he lived alone in the family's original two-room clay-plastered house. The home was an oddity at a time when most farmers in the area were building new houses and covering them with stylish red-brick veneer or brightly painted wood siding. In all respects, Yurko was considered a rather odd fellow. He was tall and awkward in appearance, with wiry blond hair, an exceptionally long, red and pimply neck, and an Adam's apple that bobbed up and down whenever he spoke. For some unexplainable reason, he had developed the strange habit of greeting everyone with a rapid "Hello, hello, hello," uttered in high-pitched nasal tones, thus earning him the nickname *Yindik*, which meant "turkey."

Although he was nearly forty, Yurko was not married. His unmarried state, however, was no indication that he was content with his life as a bachelor. On the contrary, he showed a keen interest in girls and was very fond of describing in detail his encounters with them. Not that his encounters amounted to much. "I saw Hilda in town last Saturday," he would begin. "I said to her, 'Hello, hello, hello,' and she said, 'Hello' back to me." All this was a great source of amusement to everyone who knew him, including me. That is, until I turned thirteen and Yurko began to pay extraordinary attention to me.

"Halia's getting to be a very nice girl," he commented more than once to my family. "Much nicer than some of the girls in town."

My brothers pounced on this as an opportunity to tease me incessantly. At first, I was just annoyed. Then one day, when I was alone in the front porch and about to gather up an armful of wood for the stove, I suddenly became aware of Yurko towering over me. Reeking of home-brew breath and underarm sweat, he bent toward me, awfully close.

"They're getting big," he said, staring hard at my chest. After that, I did my best to avoid him.

I didn't want to explain all this to Candy, despite her piqued curiosity. Besides, Mother needed my help immediately. After a hasty breakfast of a glass of milk and a thick slice of home-made bread spread with rhubarb jam, I filled a dishpan with warm water from the stove reservoir. The breakfast table needed to be cleared, and the cream separator had to be washed.

The large aluminum milk bowl had already taken on a cow-manure smell from the souring, grayish-white milk residue that had coagulated between the separator discs. I hated this job but dared not complain. The farm cream produced by the sixteen milk cows was a major source of revenue for our family. In the morning and the evening, the separated cream was poured into earthenware gallon jugs. They were kept cool, hanging in the waters of the spring well, until the cream truck arrived. Then the cream was transferred into large cream cans and shipped off to the creamery.

Any cream that was not stored in the earthenware jugs would be used liberally in the fabulous summer feast that Mother was intending to prepare for dinner. There would be borscht, fragrant with dill and laced with fresh, sweet cream; roasted chicken pieces, glazed in a rich flavorful cream sauce; boiled new potatoes with sautéed onions simmered in thick cream, and a big salad of chopped lettuce and green onions made luscious by the addition of dollops of sour cream.

"Do you have to do this?" Candy hung around, trying to be helpful, but she was impatient to get outdoors.

"I told you. There's a lot to do today." *City girls have no idea about some things,* I thought. In a few hours, seven hungry men and boys would sit around our table. My father, Dido, Uncle Harry, and my two older brothers Paul and Eddie would be among them. Also, Mr. Korchik, a fat, jolly neighbor who was Father's best friend. And, of course, Yurko.

I swished the separator discs in clean rinse water and shook them, jingling them harder than I needed to.

"But I really want to go outside," Candy whined. I couldn't blame her. It was a warm morning. Flies were freely buzzing in and out of the summer kitchen, some of them meeting their demise as they stuck to the strips of sticky flypaper that hung near the wood stove.

"Well, here's our chance," I said. "The reservoir is almost empty. We'll have to get more water from the well."

With galvanized buckets in hand, Candy and I set out for the spring well. We followed the worn-down path through a skunk-grass meadow that separated the house from the barnyard.

"Have you ever been kissed?" Candy asked. She was like that, blurting straight out what was on her mind.

"Of course!" I responded quickly. Of course, I *had* been kissed. For as long as I could remember, kissing was a formality associated with the comings and goings of relatives who frequented our farm. A visiting uncle, sitting on a chair in our kitchen, would inevitably beckon to whichever child stood in the doorway, listening to the conversation. "Come here. Sit on my knee." And the child would obey, sitting stiffly on his knee as requested. "Give me a *chom* (kiss)." The child would submit to his kiss and was subsequently rewarded with an Eat-More candy bar. At departure time, the kissing ritual was even more lucrative. Aunts and uncles would approach each one of us with a kiss, while discreetly pressing nickels or dimes into our palms. We gleefully hoarded them in our own secret hiding places.

"I mean, have you ever been kissed by a *boy*?" Candy asked.

"Well, no." Yurko's foul breath in my face didn't count. Not that I wanted to count it.

"Well, I have," Candy announced lightly. "There was this boy I really liked. We were at a birthday party, and he kissed me on the mouth. I liked it. I didn't wash my face for a week! Oooh! Here we are! I love this place!" Candy squealed with delight.

We had arrived at the spring well, the veritable source of life on our farm. It was the reason my grandfather had chosen to buy this farm when he arrived in Canada from Ukraine in 1930. From rivers deep underground, flowing down from the Blue Hills, the spring bubbled up and overflowed—always cool, always fresh. It provided a constant source of water for the family, for the livestock, even for the garden in times of drought. My father had encased the spring with a cement cribbing and attached a spout through which the water trickled, day and night, winter and summer, forming an ice-cold brook that meandered at will, eastward away from the farm.

"Let's have a splash party," Candy begged, "like we did last year." A splash party was the delight of all my city-girl cousins. The idea was to strip naked, stand still, and be splashed by a pail full of cold water before running off, screaming and shivering in ecstasy.

"I don't think so, Candy. Remember how we got caught?" We laughed, remembering how Paul had climbed up a tall poplar tree behind the chicken coop. He had been secretly watching us for some time before hooting like an owl to alert us of his presence. "Besides," I added, "can't you see? There are too many men around."

The first loads of hay had already been brought into the farmyard. At the edge of the aspen woods, just beyond the chicken coop, Windy and Sandy—our two brown workhorses—were just pulling up a rack bulging with hay. Paul and Eddie were perched confidently on the top of the load, pitchforks in hand, poised to transfer their sweet-smelling cargo down to the ground below, where Dido was painstakingly building a haystack.

Across the yard, another near-empty rack was parked in front of our big red barn. My father was tossing the last forkful of hay through the wide-open doors of the loft. Suddenly, a figure of a man appeared in the loft entrance. He was dressed in blue overalls and a red-checkered flannel shirt, a wide-brimmed straw hat sitting crookedly on his head. It was unmistakably Yurko. He jumped onto the rack and down to the ground.

"Oh no," I muttered. Yurko and my father were strolling toward the well. I knew why they were coming. A drinking cup always hung conveniently not far from the spout, available for anyone needing to quench his thirst.

"Is it him?" Candy asked. "Your boyfriend?"

"He's not my boyfriend!" I whispered tersely, upset with myself for not having filled my buckets earlier. I braced myself for Yurko's unsolicited attentions.

To my surprise, Yurko didn't even seem to notice me.

"Who's the girl?" he asked, eyeing my cousin.

"That's Candace, my brother's girl, from Winnipeg," my father explained as he strode off in the direction of Dido and the haystack. Now we were alone at the well with Yurko. Yurko repeatedly filled the cup from the flowing spout and took deep draughts of the cool water, his eyes all the while fastened on Candy.

Then a most unexpected thing happened. Yurko hung the cup back on its nail and approached Candy, who was standing nonchalantly at the edge of the brook, dipping her big toe in and out of the water. "Hello, hello, hello," he said. "How about a kiss?" Without waiting for a response, he planted a dusty kiss squarely on her cheek. Turning around, he strutted back to the hayrack.

For an instant, Candy stood in shock. Then, wiping her hand violently across her cheek, she cried out, "How dare he? How dare he do that?"

"I thought you like being kissed," I teased her. I was relieved that it hadn't happened to me; and, at the same time, I was aware of the irony of the moment, in light of our recent discussion.

"He's old and he's ugly. How dare he!"

It was plain that Candy's day was completely ruined. For the rest of the morning—while I scrubbed potatoes, fixed the lettuce salad, and set the table—she grumbled and plotted revenge.

"We could put salt in his borscht; lots of extra salt," she suggested.

"That wouldn't work," I told her. "Mother always sets a big bowlful of borscht in the middle of the table. Everyone helps himself."

"Well, where is he going to sit? I could spit in his teacup. Or we could put flypaper on his chair. Or we could put horse liniment on his bread. Do you have any horse liniment? I once read a story where a woman did that to get even with her husband for making fun of her cooking."

She continued in this vein until she noticed the men approaching the summer kitchen for dinner. Then Candy deserted me, retreating to the main house, where she flopped on the *pyryna* and read her Archie comic books. She refused to emerge until long after the men had left and I was half finished washing up the dishes.

"Well, how did it go?" she questioned me. "He didn't choke on a chicken bone by any chance, did he?"

"No, nothing like that happened. But he did ask about you."

"No! What did he say?"

"He just wanted to know where you were. He said you were a nice girl."

"Oooh!" Candy pulled at her hair with both hands. "We just have to do something to teach him a lesson, but I don't know what! Can you think of something?"

I wasn't much help. Candy didn't realize that she had embarked on a foray that was far beyond my experience. My mother had taught me always to be polite and respectful to grownups. Much as I despised Yurko, I would never have dared to play a trick on him.

"Let's go somewhere and figure this thing out," Candy pleaded.

I shook my head. Though it was the middle of the afternoon, I was still not free of my chores.

"We have to make lunch and take it out to the hayfield."

"But they just had dinner!" Candy pointed out.

A farm crew, laboring all day in the hot sun and parching wind, needs plenty of refreshment and fuel to keep going. My skinny, city-bred cousin, who could run around all day and hardly eat a thing, couldn't comprehend this. Nevertheless, she helped me as I made dozens of sandwiches with store-bought rye bread and thin slices of baloney. She waited, with just a touch of impatience, as I filled two half-gallon Mason jars with cold water and added sugar and packets of Freshie orange crystals to make a cooling, energizing drink.

"Carl will help you take this lunch out to the hayfield," Mother instructed us as we packed the food, along with a jar of dill pickles and a tin full of oatmeal cookies, into cardboard boxes. "But first I want you to go into the garden and get some green onions. You know how much Dido likes raw onions with his lunch."

It's funny how the simplest thing can spawn the most brilliant idea. Candy and I were in the vegetable garden, selecting the choicest green onions to add to the lunchbox, when we were distracted by a whirring sound. A flock of sparrows descended upon the lettuce patch and began poking holes in the young green leaves.

"You need a scarecrow in this garden," Candy suggested, "Last week, I saw this great movie, *The Wizard of Oz*. It had this terrific scarecrow in it. How come you don't have a scarecrow?"

"I guess there's enough of everything—for us and for the birds!" I laughed. Our vegetable garden was about the size of a city block. We had never felt the need for a scarecrow.

All of a sudden, Candy jumped up excitedly. With her hands over her head, she did a little dance, her feet almost trampling down a row of carrots.

"I've got it! I've got it! We can make a scarecrow out of him!"

"What do you mean? Who?"

"*Yerkow!*" she shouted. She couldn't quite pronounce his name the way we did. "We could make a scarecrow that looks like him! That'll teach him!"

From that moment, our day took on a whole new purpose. The adventure Candy had been seeking lay before us. As we carried the lunchboxes out to the hayfield, cutting through the cow pasture and stepping carefully around piles of cow dung, Candy and I lagged behind Carl so that he would not hear us discussing our audacious plan.

"We'll need a pair of overalls and a red-checkered flannel shirt, just like his," Candy whispered.

"I'm sure we can find an old pair of overalls somewhere—and my dad used to have a red-checkered flannel shirt. Maybe it's still in the rag box."

"What about a straw hat? Do you have one? We've got to have a straw hat!"

"No, I don't think so—but wait! There's an old yellow hat with a very wide brim hanging on a nail in the side porch. It used to be Mother's. It has flowers on it, though."

"All the better," said Candy. "We want him to look ridiculous!" Then she stopped abruptly. "Oh, oh," she muttered.

We had reached the barbed-wire fence that separated the cow pasture from the hayfield. The sweet aroma of freshly mown hay permeated our nostrils. Just beyond the fence, in plain view, Mr. Korchik's two black horses stood patiently, heads nodding sleepily, tails swishing like windshield wipers to ward off flies. Behind them was a partly filled hayrack. And Yurko was beside it, leaning against his pitchfork and mopping his forehead with a dotted red handkerchief.

"I'm not going any farther!" Candy sat on a huge granite rock and waited. I deposited my bundle in the field and fled the scene, too. Carl could bring back the empty boxes himself. I had things to do.

"How are we going to do this?" asked Candy. "What if your mother wants you to do something?"

"We have a little bit of time before supper," I assured my cousin. "We can work behind the caragana bushes, over there by the outhouse. If Mother calls me, you can say I'm in the toilet." I had used this strategy many times before, whenever I wanted time to myself.

We needn't have worried. If Mother noticed what we were up to, she never let on. In any case, by this time I had abandoned any remaining scruples about playing tricks on grownups and had thrown myself into the project completely.

Candy and I found everything that we needed in the side porch of the main house. For the next hour we worked feverishly and furtively behind the caragana bushes, constructing our scarecrow.

"It's good!" shouted Candy, when we had finished, "It's fantastic! It's the scarecrow from *The Wizard of Oz,* only dressed up in Yerkow's clothes!"

Over a simple frame fashioned out of dry poplar branches, we had arranged Father's worn-out red-checkered shirt and Paul's faded blue overalls with the torn knees. A sugar bag stuffed with rags served as a head, upon which Candy had painted a jack-o'-lantern face. For a finishing touch, we had pinned a dotted red handkerchief to the cuff of the right sleeve and attached it to the scarecrow's forehead. Mother's floppy old yellow hat with the purple flowers crowned our creation.

"It's good," I agreed. "It looks ridiculous, but it's good!"

We left our Yurko replica well hidden in the caragana bushes and rejoined Mother in the summer kitchen. There was still so much to do. Paul and Eddie had come in from the fields to help Mother with evening milking. I was left in charge of heating up the leftovers for supper, making a fresh salad, and setting the table.

It was not until Mother had brought in the milk from the barn that Candy and I dared to bring our scarecrow out of its hiding place. We positioned it just inside the gate of the gray picket fence that enclosed the yard, leaning it against the trunk of a spruce tree. From the summer kitchen, it was hidden from view; but anyone coming in from the barnyard would be sure to see it. Acting upon a last-minute inspiration, I hurriedly sneaked a pitchfork from the barn and stuck it into the ground beside the scarecrow.

The dusty sun-blackened men finally started coming in for supper. Candy and I hid behind the rain barrel to watch the procession into the yard. Father and Dido were the first to come through the gate. Father looked puzzled but said nothing. Dido didn't even seem to notice our creation. Then came Mr. Korchik, Uncle Harry, and Yurko, followed by Paul and Eddie. Mr. Korchik's hearty laugh suddenly rang in the air.

"That looks like you, Yurko," he said. At the rear, Paul and Eddie were snickering audibly.

Yurko, his face turned scarlet and his eyes cast down,

walked straight ahead toward the summer kitchen. We could see his Adam's apple bobbing up and down uncontrollably, but no sound was coming out of his throat. Candy and I turned to each other with gleeful grins and clapped our hands together.

When the supper dishes were finally put away, I sank gratefully into the grass beneath a sprawling Manitoba maple tree. The men, at last, were in a mellow mood. They sat in front of the house, drinking beer and not saying anything, lulled into silence by the soothing trickle of the spring and by the symphonies of the frogs in the marsh beyond the pasture. Uncle Harry had rolled himself a cigarette and was spewing lazy, aromatic puffs into the air.

Yurko was the first to take his leave of the gathering. He had said hardly a word over supper, and now he barely mumbled his goodbyes. Glancing nervously in the direction of the spruce tree by the picket fence, he started across the yard.

I heard Mr. Korchik mutter quietly, under his breath, *"Nash yindik peeshow na banta* (Our turkey has gone home to roost)."

It was then that I noticed that our scarecrow had fallen over and was lying down, its face in the dirt. An unexpected thought struck me with a powerful force that shattered my complacency. That was Yurko, lying there on the ground, his face in the dirt. We had done this to him, Candy and I—and all the others who had snickered behind his back. The sweet satisfaction, which had hung like a mist over the evening, suddenly dissipated, replaced by the weight of remorse. As Yurko walked limply down the driveway and out of sight, I found myself feeling genuinely sorry for him.

Candy, on the other hand, appeared to be unburdened by any feelings of remorse. She was swinging like a monkey from one of the lower limbs of the tree and singing in clear, sweet, soft tones, *"Somewhere over the rainbow / Bluebirds fly / Birds fly over the rainbow / Why then, oh why can't I?"*

157

Suddenly she let go and dropped down beside me.

"I have a fantastic idea, Halia," she said. "Let's sleep in the hayloft tonight!"

I smiled at my cousin. The sun was rising again in my soul.

"Let's do that," I said. "But first, let's put our scarecrow away."

Veechnaya Pamyat

(Eternal Memory)

SONJA DUNN

Too young at five
to know
my mother's eyes
were forever shuttered.

Lone pine coffin
in the hollow room
a vague memory now,
picked up
by six strong men
and carried across
the highway to St. Teresa's church.

No hearse
no cars
only a poor procession
Ukrainian immigrants
chanting
"Veechnaya Pamyat"
the eternal memory dirge.

1970s

Changing Graves

SONJA DUNN

This story is based on a real incident that happened to my relatives. In some ways it was fitting that the bizarre old-world request, that a loved one should be exhumed and the coffin moved to be closer to other relatives, should end in such black comedy.

"Dust from the top of the hill spits on my poor Vasyl's grave and makes anthills," my Aunt Toshka said to my Uncle Mykola.

"*Mykolchoo, Mykolchoo.*" She always used the diminutive when she spoke to her brother.

"Vasyl's grave is in a very bad place. It's on a slant, and when it rains, the rushing torrents wash away all the candles and the flowers that I've planted. The sod gets wet. And when I kneel to pray, my arthritis bothers me. Besides, why should my poor husband be all by himself at Prospect Cemetery, when Auntie Maria, Cousin Tomko, Uncle Yousip, and all our friends and relatives are buried at Park Lawn?"

From her deathbed she pleaded, "Promise me that after I'm gone, you'll have his coffin moved, and bury us both side by side at Park Lawn."

160

At the funeral of Oksana Kuryliw's uncle, Petro; procession started from his home in the village of Potochyska and stretched approximately three blocks to the cemetery. Taken in the 1970s

This sounded like quite a simple procedure at the time, and Uncle Mykola assured her that he would fulfill her request. The younger family members—those who had been born in Canada—thought it was a crazy idea, but my uncle pointed out that graves were often moved in Ukraine, and it wouldn't present a problem. Little did he know! But "a promise made is a debt unpaid," and after my Aunt Toshka's death and burial, the time came to transfer Vasyl's casket to Park Lawn.

Uncle Mykola soon found, after many phone calls, that this project in Canada was somewhat more complicated than in Ukraine. There was more to this than just digging up Uncle Vasyl from his resting place of fifteen years and dropping him in his new residence. There was also a large tombstone to consider. The cemetery officials informed my uncle that he would need to contact the health department, the grave digger, and the actual casket exhumers. We would need a vehicle to transport the casket, several men with other necessary equipment, and a priest. There were permits to be procured, and the timing had to be arranged to suit all the participants.

Toronto was at its bleakest on that November day of 1992, when the deed was to be done. Snow swirled around tombstones that seemed to be restless in the nearly frozen ground. It was not an ideal time for picnics.

Uncle Mykola, his daughter, my cousin Martha, and I met with the entire crew at Prospect Cemetery at high noon. Uncle Vasyl's mud-covered casket lay at the bottom of the already-dug-out pit. When the workmen began the disinterment, they found it was no easy task. The side walls of the pit were slightly narrower than the casket, which was covered with a rough box, or rigid outer container. The workmen pushed, pulled, gesticulated, huffed, and puffed to no avail. The box wouldn't budge. The slippery slope of the hill was also a hindrance, and the crew kept slipping, sliding, and falling. The disgruntled men swore in languages I didn't recognize.

Up to this point, the atmosphere had been somewhat somber, but now the health inspector, the priest, and my Uncle Mykola began yelling out advice on how to get the coffin out of the grave.

"Put the box upright!" one of the men shouted.

"The sucker won't budge on this side!"

"Then slant it!"

"Pull harder on the straps!"

"Careful now, you'll crack it open. We don't want any leaks here," urged the health inspector.

What was to be a reverent affair was turning into a fiasco. In exasperation and disapproval, my uncle cried out, *"Chysta comedia!* (Sheer comedy!)" His attempts at maintaining some dignity were failing. Martha and I suppressed giggles while my uncle paced back and forth, muttering under his breath, suggesting that the men were incompetent, disorganized, and didn't have the right equipment for the job. There was a lot of looking down in the hole and head shaking. The consensus was that the fault lay with the diggers, who hadn't dug the walls wide enough.

"I have an important private baptism this evening," announced the confused old priest. "There won't be time to bless the grave at Park Lawn unless they speed it up," he added in Ukrainian. But my worried uncle was undeterred. He found a shovel in the dump truck that was to have transported Vasyl's coffin, and he began to chip away at the sides of the excavation.

"It's no use. We have to tilt the coffin upright," said the fellow who seemed to be the boss. The wind began to toss the snow and leaves around more vigorously, and it was turning colder and darker.

Two long planks had been placed at the graveside, presumably so that the casket could slide to the bottom of the incline and be lifted onto the truck. Unfortunately, during the activities the planks had moved about. When the scummy casket, covered with mud, roots, and grubs, was finally fished out, upright, it stood on its end, teetered unsteadily, and fell on a plank upside down. Then it suddenly took flight down the hill.

The casket slid downhill, first on the plank and then on the frozen grass, escaping with everyone in hot pursuit. The workmen were in the lead, shouting as they ran; the health inspector lost his footing and slid down the hill, unceremoniously; the breathless old priest ran with his black chasuble flapping in the wind; and the few other bewildered bystanders joined the entourage. It reminded me of an old Laurel and Hardy escapade.

Martha and I found it difficult to keep from laughing outright. My uncle, who could see no humor in the situation, was calling on God and all the saints to have mercy on us. It was an unusual sight.

Gravity being what it is, Uncle Vasyl sailed down the grassy slope in his coffin and came to rest at the foot of the dump truck. The men turned the casket right side up, with great difficulty, and the embarrassed health inspector conscientiously inspected the exterior and departed. The workmen—who by now were cold, tired, and grouchy—hoisted their load onto the dump truck in triumph. Behind us, up on the hill, the elaborate tombstone, which was to be moved at a later date, stood forlornly at the head of the empty hole.

Our ragtag procession began with the dump truck, with my uncle, who insisted on guarding the coffin because there was no tail gate, standing in the back with the coffin. The reluctant priest, the workers' car, and Martha and I brought up the rear as we slowly inched along snow-covered Toronto streets in the midst of rush hour.

Unexpectedly, our short procession got involved with another funeral. What must the bereaved have thought when a dump truck joined their group? Later, my uncle explained that the original funeral director had told him that his hearses would be all tied up on that day. Martha and I suspected that there was an entirely different reason.

After many red lights, left turns, and life-threatening maneuvers, I managed to get separated from the others. Finally, late, and under a darkening sky, Martha and I reached our destination at Park Lawn.

We found the workers trying to lower the coffin into the new digs. Alas, the sides of the new grave were too narrow. The coffin wouldn't fit. They tried this way and that, pushing and twisting without success.

Finally, a vociferous command came from the man who

seemed to be the boss. "Just push the god-damned thing in the god-damned hole!"

Placing a boot on top of the casket, he put his full weight on it, and he and the casket both slid sideways into the excavation. There were more expletives and shouts as he scrambled up the sides of the open grave. The nearly frozen priest, his black chasuble now snow-covered and still flapping about in the wind, hurriedly gave the final blessing and departed. We were amazed when he called the deceased Yousip instead of Vasyl— but the poor old fellow was rather confused after the chain of events, and one couldn't blame him.

In a matter of moments the dump truck, the cars, and the people departed with great speed. Uncle Mykola, Cousin Martha, and I were left at the new grave site, staring down at Vasyl's casket. It was covered with dirt, roots, and whatever other detritus had accumulated over the fifteen years it had lain in its original resting place.

In the spring, when Nadia and Boris Moroz came to tend their father's neighboring grave, much to their surprise Vasyl Kostetski's tombstone had disappeared, and in its place was a gaping hole. Vasyl and his coffin had vanished from Prospect Cemetery forever!

> There's a grave in the meadow
> She speaks to the wind,
> "Blow gently, wind
> So that I may not wither."
> —*Traditional poem*

Before Glasnost, Oy Jovarish

(Before Glasnost, Hey Friend)

SONJA DUNN

The Ukrainians
are singing tonight
in the basement
of St. Vladymir's
it's the same old song
the constant one
that they sing
about Ukraine
not dead yet
and they sing about
her glory and freedom
and they sing about
her brothers and sisters
always loyal
and they sing
about the future
not in any poetic phrases

just plain talk
about how Ukraine's foes
will be vanquished
under this new Glasnost

Oy tovarish
do you believe
what the Ukrainians
are singing
tonight?

2004

Christmas Missed

PAULETTE MACQUARRIE

*I like stories with contrasts; the Orange Revolution
provided many, particularly between the political awareness
of young people in North America and those in Eastern
Europe. There was also a contrast between the peacefulness
of the Orange Revolution and other revolutions.*

*I was also struck by the contrast between the behavior
of the Canadian government today, ensuring voting
fairness in Ukraine's election, and the Canadian government during World War I, when it took the vote away
from Ukrainian immigrants. The treatment of Ukrainian
immigrants in Canada during the First World War is
seldom mentioned in Canadian history books, and I
wanted to raise awareness of it.*

Daniel Jones squinted through the store window at
the display of electronics, hoping he'd finally found the perfect
gift for his dad. What a chore Christmas shopping was! They
never gave him any clues—probably because they both had
good jobs and were able to buy pretty much whatever they
wanted. And they did. Christmas was a bit of a farce, anyway.

Orange Revolution, 2004. From the exhibit, "Voices of a Nation," showcased in Winnipeg, Manitoba

Despite all the complaints about the commercialization of Christmas, their tree always groaned with gifts on Christmas morning, and Daniel had yet to experience a church service with his parents.

He was at his wits' end, trying to think of something cool so he wouldn't hear those Christmas spirit-killing words, "the thought was nice" again this year. The Body Shop was straight ahead, but Daniel walked right past it. He'd bought Body Shop perfume for his mom last year, and he would never forget how he felt, one gray day in January, when he saw it fall out of the garbage bag. Mom loved her expensive designer-label perfume. Maybe he'd just go to Canadian Tire. All three of them had a car, and he wanted new floor mats for his, anyway.

A group of laughing and chattering people coming up behind him interrupted Daniel's tedious task. Although he didn't recognize the language they were speaking, he could see that they were excited about something. As they rushed past him, Daniel quickly checked out the three girls in the group. Nice! They were wearing orange scarves, though—and so were the guys. Weird. They did brighten up the typically gray November day, but orange wasn't exactly a common color on Vancouver's trendy Robson Street.

Intrigued, he decided to follow them. The Christmas shopping could wait. As he hurried after them, he heard the familiar dull drone of crowd noises getting louder and clearer. His heart dropped as he realized they must be going to some protest rally. *Duh!* Guess that's what the picket signs were about.

Daniel shook his head in self-disgust. The shopping must have dulled his mind. You'd think that with all the anti-government protests his parents had dragged him to, the signs would have been a dead giveaway. Then again, he thought with a grin, why would he be looking at signs when there were girls in tight jeans?

When the Vancouver Art Gallery came into view, so did hundreds more orange scarves. Cars honked at people waving blue-and-yellow flags. Daniel noticed some signs, written in English, with slogans about the elections in Ukraine. But most fascinating of all was the look on the protesters' faces. Excitement! What kind of a demonstration was this, anyway? Weren't protesters supposed to be angry and outraged?

"Hey, Daniel!"

"Terry!" Daniel hadn't expected to find any familiar faces in this crowd. He broke into a big grin when he saw Terry Kowal sprinting toward him, waving a blue-and-yellow flag.

"What are you doing here?" Daniel asked. "And what's with all the orange?"

Terry laughed a bit self-consciously, but Daniel noticed a new air of excitement about his normally reserved and studious friend.

"Well, my parents were coming to this rally, and they dragged me along," explained Terry. At Daniel's skeptical look, he flushed slightly and looked away for a few seconds.

"Okay, I'll admit I wanted to come," he said. "This is history in the making. There's a revolution going on in Ukraine, and hundreds of thousands of people are coming out of the woodwork to kick out the government."

Daniel snorted. "Yeah, well, my parents didn't have much luck with our government here." Daniel recalled his parents' bitterness that the unions weren't able to bring down the government in that strike last spring, and it was humungous compared to this rally. "What do you expect to do about some third-world country? And anyway, isn't the Ukraine part of Russia?"

Terry sighed and rolled his eyes.

"How many times do I have to drum it into your thick skull that it's *Ukraine*, not *the* Ukraine?" He pretended to hit Daniel on the head with his flagpole. "And no, Ukraine is definitely not part of Russia; it's a sovereign country. And that's what this is all about!"

"Hey, take it easy!" Daniel pretended to duck. "I thought you said this was about democracy?"

"Exactly," said Terry. "The election on November twenty-first was fixed by corrupt government officials who want power at all costs. That's not exactly democratic." Terry pointed his sign at the protesters. "Listen."

Daniel couldn't understand the words, but he could feel the rhythm of the chant.

"*Yoo-shchen-ko!*" One. Two. Three. Over and over again.

"That's the name of the opposition leader," Terry said, flipping his scarf back over his shoulder.

"Yes, Yushchenko," said a deep voice. Daniel turned and looked into another pair of blue eyes the exact shade of Terry's. "Where's your orange scarf?" the man asked.

"Oh, hi, Dr. Kowal," said Daniel. He liked Terry's parents and siblings and was envious of their tight-knit family. Not to mention the food! He could almost feel himself drool every time he thought of Mrs. Kowal's homemade perogies.

"I followed some people here." He looked around, but they had melted into the crowd. "They were wearing orange, too. What's with that, anyway?"

"Orange is the color of Yushchenko's campaign, and it's become the color of Ukrainian democracy," Dr. Kowal explained. "And look what I just happen to have in my pocket."

With a magician's flourish, he pulled out an orange scarf and handed it to Daniel.

"We'll be here for another hour or so. If you're not too busy, you're welcome to join us for dinner afterward."

The next weekend, Daniel returned the favor. On Sunday afternoon, he and Terry went to pick up Daniel's great-grandfather for the Jones family's monthly Sunday dinner. Daniel always volunteered to pick Gramps up. Sometimes Daniel would even pop over to the nursing home for a visit on his own. It wasn't a very exciting place, but he felt as if he was doing something good. Gramps had always been a big part of Daniel's life. He told great stories, and he didn't act his age at all. For someone who was ninety-one, he was pretty cool.

"At least the rain has let up today," Terry remarked as they walked from the parking lot to the lobby.

"As if you'd notice," teased Daniel. "You've been glued to your computer!"

Terry elbowed Daniel as they got into the elevator. "I found a site with up-to-the-minute coverage of the situation in Ukraine. It looks like we won't need to hold any more rallies here."

The elevator pinged, and the door opened.

"Maybe you can tell Gramps about it," said Daniel as they walked down the corridor to his grandfather's room. "He's pretty interested in politics." *And I, definitely, am not,* he added silently.

The door was slightly ajar, and the boys heard the familiar sounds of a TV news report. Daniel rapped on the door and pushed it open.

"Hey, Gramps!" Daniel crossed the floor and gave his great-grandfather a quick peck on the top of his bald head.

"Hello, lads," said Allan MacGregor, a grin lighting up his wrinkled face. "What are you two doing visiting a boring old man on a beautiful Sunday afternoon?"

"Hi, Mr. MacGregor," said Terry, shaking the old man's hand. "Who better to spend time with than my favorite surrogate grandfather?"

"Ach, there's a smooth talker!" He shook his head in mock disgust, and, setting his book on the table beside his chair, got up and shuffled toward the small fridge at the other end of the room. "Would you be liking a drink, lads? There's root beer or apple juice."

Daniel took two cans and joined Terry on the sofa. There was a companionable lull in the conversation, broken only by the sound of pop cans being opened and the drone of the TV newscaster.

"Hey!" Terry's eyes flew to the TV. "What's this?"

"Huh?" said Daniel. "What's what?"

"Shut up and listen!" Terry leaned forward, staring intensely at the TV. The reporter was saying that the Canadian government was calling for observers to go to Ukraine and monitor the election rerun. "This is what I was telling you about on the way here!"

The news story was a repeat, so Allan MacGregor sat back and enjoyed the sight of the two lads. He liked his great-grandson's friend. He was a good influence on Daniel, just as Feodr had been on him. Maybe with this Orange Revolution, he'd impress upon Daniel how important the vote was. Terry looked remarkably like Feodr, except that his wrists were smooth and unscarred. Allan's gut still burned as he recalled how his relatives had referred to his friend and mentor as "that stupid bohunk" and how Feodr had meekly accepted their prejudice without protest.

"Hah!" said Terry, sitting back after the newscast ended. He was smiling hugely. "Just watch Mom and Dad go!"

"As should you, lad!"

Daniel stared at his grandfather, puzzled at the vehemence in his voice. Was he forgetting what time of year it was?

"They'd miss Christmas," said Daniel.

"Ach! There'll be more Christmases!" Gramps thumped his can on the table next to his easy chair. "But this revolution— aye, this is a once-in-a-lifetime proposition."

He switched off the TV with a snap of the remote and settled back into his chair. Daniel could feel the intensity of his great-grandfather's gaze, although it was directed at Terry. Outside, the traffic swished and an ambulance siren went off, but inside the seconds ticked by silently.

As Allan MacGregor regarded Terry, images of his old friend Feodr flashed in his mind. He recalled how Feodr had considered the right to vote precious. Feodr had taught the pampered young MacGregor how to put his back into his work on Uncle Alistair's farm. He'd also taught him how to cuss in Ukrainian, and how to produce moonshine that rivaled the finest vodka money could buy.

Their friendship ended on Election Day in the year 1926. It was in the middle of harvest season, and even the threat of losing his job would not keep Feodr from exercising his right to vote.

"You want fire me, fine!" The usually docile and almost obsequious Feodr glared at Alistair with open defiance. "I going vote!"

His last memory of Feodr was of him stalking out the door, cap in hand, toward the wagon that was taking voters to the polls.

Allan MacGregor never forgave his uncle. Alistair was one of those bigots who'd resented the arrival of hard-working immigrants from Eastern Europe; he had no qualms about labeling them "enemy aliens" when war broke out. Racial profiling—wasn't that what it was called today? Of course, today they didn't dare set up internment camps for people who happened to have been born in the wrong place. And he couldn't imagine anyone today insisting their town was "entitled" to the free labor of internees, as his uncle and other relatives did, even years after the abominable camps had been finally closed. Apparently Uncle Alistair had also been dead set against giving women the vote but changed his mind in 1917. That year, Prime Minister Borden was re-elected by taking the vote away from the east European men who had supported the opposition Liberals, and by enfranchising women who were related to servicemen. The only thing Allan remembered about 1917 was the train ride he'd taken through the Rockies. He'd just turned four, and he and his parents were en route to his uncle's farm in Saskatchewan. They'd all had been blissfully unaware of the work camps, not far from where the train passed by, where men like Feodr worked at the end of a bayonet.

"Maybe, just maybe," Allan said out loud, "this Orange Revolution will give Canada a chance to exonerate itself."

Daniel and Terry exchanged puzzled glances.

"What do you mean, Gramps?"

Allan looked from one lad to the other. One day soon he'd tell them about Feodr. Perhaps then Daniel would realize how precious the right to vote in a democracy was. But for now, the future held more interest for them than the past.

"Canada is always sending election observers to countries around the world," the old man replied. "Yet so far it's been private citizens—people like your parents," he nodded to Terry, "paying their own way to Ukraine to monitor this election. It's high time our government joined them."

Daniel let Gramps and Terry out of the car as he parked his Mazda beside his mother's SUV in the garage. He hoped it was a good idea to invite Terry to dinner this Sunday. It might have been better to break the news to his parents when they were alone. They liked Terry well enough, since his dad was a doctor and all. But ever since the Orange Revolution had become the big news story of the year, Daniel had come to realize that his parents held political views that were different from those that Terry and his parents held—and from those Daniel and Gramps held, too.

Ever since that rally at the art gallery, he and Terry had spent every spare minute watching Internet videos from Ukraine. Terry provided simultaneous translation of the news reports. The images burned in Daniel's memory—wall-to-wall people chanting in the freezing cold, endless orange tents, rows of grim-faced guards in riot gear, bonfires lighting up dark winter nights, smiling women, and pretty girls handing out bowls of borscht to cold and cheerful demonstrators. Even though he had always disliked politics, he began to think that he might like to be an election observer, too—like Terry's parents. Or just camp out in the tent city with Terry. What an experience it would be! This Orange Revolution was history in the making, and he intended to be part of it. At nineteen, he didn't need his parents' permission to go, but he'd like their blessing. And, maybe some help with the airfare.

"Over my dead body!" Mike Jones glared at his son. Daniel stared down at his plate. He knew it was pointless to argue with his dad when he had that look on his face.

"You can't be serious!" His mother, Sarah, was talking to

Daniel, but looking at Terry in a weird way.

"Why not, Mom?" Daniel took a deep breath. Be calm. Be adult. "You and Dad are always protesting the government, and it's pretty obvious the Ukrainians have way more to protest than anyone in Canada does."

"Aye, indeed. Why not?" Gramps brought his fist down on the table.

Out of the corner of his eye, Daniel noticed his mother jump ever so slightly. Gramps might be old and frail, but he still commanded respect.

"It's too dangerous," said Sarah.

Daniel gaped at his mother. She had to be kidding! He'd be going with Terry and his parents, for crying out loud.

"We can't afford it!" Mike snapped, sawing at his meat.

Gramps snorted, tilting his head toward Sarah's collection of Swarovski crystal in the expensive teak-and-glass corner cabinet.

"But ye can afford Cuba?" Sarah had the grace to blush. "And there was no danger sending your boy to poke around there?"

Gramps would never let his parents forget that they were supporting a bloody dictator by sending him on that school trip last year.

"That's different!" said Mike, his face set in the grim lines that Daniel always saw in the faces of people at the protest rallies. "Besides, he'd miss Christmas."

"What utter hypocrisy!" Allan MacGregor threw his napkin onto his half-finished meal.

Planting his hands on the table to pull himself up, he leaned over and glared at Daniel's parents.

"I'll see to it Daniel experiences this revolution," he said, his eyes blazing steel. "You keep Christmas in your own way."

Daniel tossed every pair of socks he owned into his duffel bag.

He'd never spent a winter outside of Vancouver, and Dr. Kowal said this winter was colder than usual in Ukraine. He looked dubiously at the orange scarf draped over the back of his chair. Terry said they were the height of fashion in Ukraine, and that Ukrainian girls found guys in orange sexy. He tossed it in, along with the orange toque Mrs. Kowal had knitted for him.

He was really going to Ukraine! Daniel carefully arranged his visa and passport in the soft leather case his mother had given him last night after she had hastily prepared an early Christmas dinner. He'd been surprised when Sarah had come home at noon with a pre-stuffed turkey from the supermarket. A few days ago, she'd been going on about the violence that always broke out at political uprisings, and how violence was inevitable with all those supposedly racist, and anti-Semitic, Ukrainian ultra-nationalist protesters. Maybe she finally started listening to the news instead of to her sour-faced friends, who were always protesting something or other. Or maybe the Christmas spirit struck early. Whatever. He was just glad his parents weren't upset anymore.

Daniel slung his bag over his shoulder just as the doorbell rang. Terry stood on the doorstep, grinning like a fool, and Daniel could see Dr. Kowal in the car, waiting to take them to the airport. Terry's parents had been selected by the Canadian government to be election observers and would be leaving next week. In the meantime, Daniel and Terry would be on their own in Kyiv until after the election was over.

"You all packed, hon?" Sarah came down the wide staircase, tightening the belt on her bathrobe.

"Sure am!" Daniel leaned down and gave his mother a hug, holding her for several seconds. She was doing a real lousy job of trying not to look worried.

"Don't forget this, son," Mike said, coming into the foyer with a package in his hand. It was the voltage adapter for his cell phone. "Make sure you use it."

Daniel stuffed the device into his bag.

"Thanks, Dad. I will." He hugged his father quickly and then gave both his parents a smile that matched his friend's.

Daniel was surprised at all the high-rises in Kyiv; he'd expected something bleak and Orwellian. The drive into Kyiv reminded Daniel of the drive to Burnaby Mountain, and he wondered briefly if there'd be snow at home this Christmas. He shivered, impatient to get inside, as Terry paid the cab driver. If they were going to be standing around in this cold for days on end, he'd be wearing every one of those wool socks he'd packed.

Terry slapped Daniel's back as they got off the elevator.

"Let me do the talking," he said with a smirk. "You just smile and nod."

Daniel whacked Terry back and gave him an evil look. Being unilingual, he couldn't do much else. He'd be sticking close to Terry on this trip. Then again, you didn't always need words to communicate, especially with girls. He could hardly wait to meet Terry's twin cousins, Olenka and Oksana, sweet-looking identical honey blondes with perfect bodies. Terry said his photo didn't do them justice.

A tall, elegant woman opened the apartment door with a delighted little squeal and enveloped Terry in a big hug before kissing him full on the lips. Daniel had expected...what? A pleasantly plump human *matrushka* doll, smelling of fried onions and butter? Daniel stood back as Terry chatted with the woman and introduced her to Daniel as Nadia, his cousin. She shook Daniel's hand formally, but smiled warmly as she pulled him into the apartment. A thin young man, who looked about their age, rose from the sofa to greet them. Yuriy would take them to Independence Square after they'd settled in and had a bowl of hot, homemade soup. Nadia was preparing a supper of bread, smoked meat, and sauerkraut salad to take along. She gave Daniel and Terry a hopeful look as they scarfed down their soup. Maybe they could convince the twins to leave the tent city and spend some time with their mother.

It was almost dusk by the time they reached Independence Square. Daniel already recognized it by its Ukrainian name, *Maidan Nezolazhnosty*. Man, these names were something else. Fortunately, everyone just called it Maidan. All those names of the revolution, though, mostly ending in *enko* and *chuk*, were all tangled up in his head. Terry assured him he'd figure out who was who, after a day or two at Maidan.

Daniel was still game to learn a few words in Ukrainian, though. He had no trouble learning how to say yes (*tak*) and no (*ni*), but Terry had cracked up at his attempts to pronounce their Ukrainian names.

"*Ta-RAS*," said Terry. "Roll the *R*, like your Gramps does!"

Daniel had an easier time with his own Ukrainian moniker, *Danylo*, once he got used to placing the stress on the middle syllable.

They got off at Khreshchatyk metro station and walked past the evangelical free concert, set up just outside. Terry translated the banner over the tent—it was a Bible verse about God healing the peoples' land if they'd just seek his face. According to Yuriy, several prayer tents were set up in the tent city. He and the twins went to the Kyiv Orthodox tent because it had a cupola and was more like a real church.

Music blared everywhere, creating an atmosphere that was part revolution and part rock festival. Daniel commented on the lack of drugs and alcohol—no disorderly behavior, no zombies with glazed eyes, no stench of stale booze.

"Serious revolutionaries need to stay sober," Terry translated Yuriy's response.

The crowds were smaller than they had been earlier in the

month. Both Yushchenko and his rival Yanukhovych—the shill who had been installed by the detested outgoing President Kuchma—were on the campaign trail. The rigged election had been officially invalidated, and a new election date had been confirmed. Many protesters had gone back to their lives, confident that the next election would be fair. Many others, however, vowed to stay put until Yushchenko's victory was assured.

Khreshchatyk Street, Kyiv's main street, was still an ocean of orange ribbons, scarves, balloons, and even an artificial orange Christmas tree. And of course, miles of orange tents. The bits of contrasting color—the blue-and-yellow Ukrainian flag, the black garb of Eastern Christian clerics, the grey-and-brown food stalls—reminded Daniel of sailboats dotting the rich blue of Burrard Inlet.

Yuriy took them into a tent occupied by a middle-aged peasant named Vasyl, from western Ukraine. Although the tent was surrounded by stacks of firewood, the inside was quite homey—with a table, kerosene stove, and a sizable supply of canned meat and fruit. No, Vasyl hadn't seen the twins today, but they'd come around yesterday and brought him some hot chai.

The closer they got to Maidan, the louder the music got. It was mostly hip-hop and rock, but occasionally they'd hear a Ukrainian folk tune. Daniel lost count of the number of times he'd heard *"Razom nas bahato"* (Together we are many, we cannot be defeated). What an anthem for a revolution!

Maidan was dominated by a huge pillar, atop which was a golden statue of a woman in traditional Ukrainian dress. She seemed to beam down at the mass of humanity, chanting and waving flags and banners. Among the ubiquitous, orange *Yes* and Yushchenko flags were Canadian and American flags, Solidarity banners from Poland, and banners from other East European countries. One banner had a picture of a face that

Daniel found vaguely familiar.

"Che Guevara for Yushchenko," Terry translated the slogan.

"No way!" Daniel hooted. "Mom and Dad will never believe it!" He started to ask Terry if they could go and talk to the guy holding the banner, but Yuriy was pulling both of them in the opposite direction. He'd spotted the twins.

"Olenka! Oksana!" Daniel wondered how anyone could hear Yuriy, much less see him, but two girls suddenly sandwiched Yuriy and kissed him on each cheek. Daniel recognized them from the photos Terry had shown him last week. It would be easier to tell them apart now. Oksana's hair was braided with the inevitable orange ribbon, but Olenka's was short and spiky, and dyed a bright orange!

One of the bands was setting up and warming up the crowd before the politicians started giving speeches. The middle-aged lead singer exhorted the crowd to get their hands up and wave. People all over Maidan waved and began to chant, *"Yushchenko, nash president!"* (Yushchenko is our president!) They were too far away to see the stage, but didn't miss much because of the huge screens above it, and the superb sound system.

They stayed until the early hours, then went back with Yuriy to the apartment. The girls came, too. They wanted a shower and some quiet time with their Canadian cousin—and to get to know his English friend better.

The days passed in a high-energy blur of music, speeches, and exuberant faces. Most of the people were young, but there were little kids and lots of old people, too. When the crowd yelled "Yushchenko!" or "Down with Kuchma!" age was irrelevant. Everyone was united in anger and outrage. Daniel never sensed any personal danger, though. The protestors saved their anger for the corrupt regime that was ruining their country.

Terry seemed to feel obligated to act as his personal interpreter, so Daniel often used calling home as a convenient excuse to wander off on his own and give Terry some space. It wasn't unusual to hear English spoken at Maidan, and since he had a small Canadian flag sticking out of his backpack, language wasn't an issue. Besides, he always seemed to meet up with Terry, Yuriy, or one of the twins whenever he needed to.

Daniel was surprised at how many people his own age were so passionate and knowledgeable about politics and world affairs, and so eager to debate. The conversations he was used to hearing at home seemed so shallow and trivial by comparison. The most important thing to most of his friends was what had happened on the latest reality TV program, or where to find the best pizza.

He'd been pulled into debates over who was responsible for the poisoning that had so dramatically changed Yushchenko's movie-star looks—was it Kuchma or the Russian government? Was it more important for Ukraine to join the European Union or NATO first? Would making Russian an official language harm the renaissance of the Ukrainian language? How could Ukraine move closer to the West and still stay close to Russia? It was embarrassing not to be able to contribute much to the conversation, but his new friends were happy enough to broaden his knowledge.

Christmas Day was weird. December twenty-fifth was the last day of the election campaign; just another day on the calendar here. But on December twenty-fourth, Terry's relatives took them to the opera to see the *Nutcracker Suite*. Tickets were ridiculously cheap, around one dollar per person, and they thought it would be nice in case their Canadian guests were missing their English Christmas.

Election Day came and went without incident. A few news reports hinted that there might be trouble from anti-Yushchenko elements, but none materialized.

Two days after the elections, Yanukhovich still refused to

concede defeat gracefully, despite the indisputable results of 52% to 44% in Yushchenko's favor. That didn't stop the crowds, back in full force at Maidan, from reveling in their victory. It was like the best rock concert Daniel could imagine. He had no idea how people managed to dance, with everyone packed together like jelly beans in a jar. There was no shortage of girls willing to dance, but Daniel reserved the slow ones for Olenka.

After dark, Yushchenko spoke to his supporters, praising the people and giving them the credit for creating a new era of democracy. He lit a candle, symbolizing hope for their country, and then lit candles held by his family and supporters on stage. A few minutes later, all of Maidan was awash in the gentle glow of a million candles, and in a chorus of freedom sung by a million voices. Daniel didn't know the words, but he swayed with the crowd, holding his candle in one hand and Olenka's hand with the other.

Thanks, Gramps, he mouthed silently. "I wouldn't have missed this for the world."

"Okay, can we open our presents now?"

Daniel's dad chuckled and suggested to his wife that they wait awhile for dessert. Daniel felt like he was ten years old again. Except this year he was more interested in the gifts he was giving than in those he was receiving. Okay, he thought, smiling to himself, maybe just as interested was closer to the truth.

He gazed in wonder at the packages gleaming under the twinkling tree. It was a week after Mom usually put away all the Christmas decorations. Daniel remembered his conversation with Gramps on the drive from the nursing home. Gramps said that Daniel's parents had told him that Christmas just didn't seem right without Daniel there, so they would celebrate it properly after he got home. His mom had even cooked a *real* turkey dinner, and Daniel swallowed hard remembering the look in her eyes when he'd thanked her for cooking such an awesome meal.

"Go ahead, son," Mike nodded to Daniel to hand out the gifts. He picked up one that felt like a thick book and saw his name on the tag. He wasn't a big reader, and his parents and Gramps knew that. They also never failed to give him gifts that delighted him. Putting aside his curiosity, he picked up another package and handed it to his mother.

Sarah pulled an elegant orange shawl out of the tissue paper in the gift box, gasping in delight as she stroked the fine cashmere.

"It's a pashmina," Daniel said, silently thanking Olenka for insisting on helping him find souvenirs of the Orange Revolution to bring home. She'd known exactly what to get and where to get it.

Daniel passed a package to his father and watched him unwrap a large orange banner. Daniel struggled to keep a straight face as his dad gaped at the image above the Cyrillic lettering.

"Che Guevara?" He looked at Daniel, incredulous, then broke into laughter that brought tears to his eyes. "My son the revolutionary!"

Daniel grinned at his father, then at Gramps as his great-grandfather unwrapped a hinged picture frame containing three photos from Maidan. He seemed particularly taken with the one of Daniel and Terry at the base of that huge pillar, surrounded by hordes of smiling orange-clad protesters.

His father softly cleared his throat, so Daniel reached eagerly for the last gift under the tree. His jaw dropped as he opened a photo album that chronicled the life of his family. He didn't even blush at his baby pictures; there were naked baby pictures of his parents, too. But the ones that fascinated him most were the black-and-white photos.

"We missed ye so on Christmas Day, laddie," said Gramps, his voice gruff but his eyes soft.

Daniel had a vision of Gramps and his parents around the dining room table, photos spilling out of old shoeboxes in a kaleidoscope of memories, as they painstakingly created a gift that he would cherish forever.

Hugging their treasures, the three of them sat in the soft glow of the tree, smiling at each other. They might have been celebrating Christmas a bit late, but they hadn't missed it after all.

The Gift

SONJA DUNN

Amid simmering samovars
the somber colors
of the designer scarf
you gave me
that were not
in my fashion palette
fit in so well.

Those Ukrainian flowers
purple asters
and marigolds
were reminiscent
of our garden walks.

You never made it
to Ukraine
but your echoing voice
was in the beehives
and windmills.

Orange Revolution, 2004. From the exhibit,
"Voices of a Nation," showcased in Winnipeg,
Manitoba

About the Authors

CORNELIA BILINSKY
Author of "Candy's Revenge"

Cornelia (Mikolayenko) Bilinsky has fond memories of growing up on the farm that her grandparents and parents carved out of the bush and swamp of a half section of land near the Duck Mountains of Manitoba's Parkland Region. One of seven children, Cornelia remembers her childhood as a mixture of hard work and the simple pleasures of country living. One of her particular joys was attending a one-room country school two miles from home. The school actually had two rooms: a classroom and a small library. Cornelia read every book in that library, lugging them home one at a time and devoting every spare moment to reading—sometimes sneaking into the outhouse or reading under the bed covers.

Cornelia's love of reading and writing inspired her to pursue a career as an English teacher. After completing her studies at the University of Manitoba, she taught secondary school English in her hometown of Ethelbert, Manitoba. She also taught English to new Canadians in a community college in St. Catharines, Ontario. Since 1981, Cornelia has been involved in a ministry within the Ukrainian Catholic Church. She has focused on religious education for children and has created many stories, plays, and songs in an effort to bring to life Ukrainian religious and cultural heritage.

189

NATALIA BUCHOK
Author of "A Bar of Chocolate"

Natalia Buchok was born and raised in Hamilton, Ontario. She was born into a Ukrainian family. Her father was a displaced person, who had come to Canada from Europe after World War II. Her mother is a first-generation Canadian of Ukrainian descent, who was chided for dating someone "just off the boat."

Natalia was very active in the Ukrainian community as a child and teenager. She attended the University of Toronto, where she obtained a B.A. in Art History. She went on to obtain a B.A. in Psychology from York University, and then completed a Master of Social Work from the University of Toronto. She has lived and worked in the southern U.S. and in the Middle East. She now works as a child and family therapist in Oakville, Ontario, where she lives, teaches Middle Eastern dancing, and writes.

Natalia has always been an avid reader. She says that she used to bore her school friends at recess by telling them the details of the latest book she was reading. As a child, she used to make up stories, but had never thought she was good enough to actually write one. She discovered that she loved writing, however, and hasn't put down her laptop since. She has a great admiration for all the writers who came before her, especially those who didn't have the luxury of computers.

SONJA DUNN

Author of "Violin," "Memories of Volodymyr Serotiuk's Birthday," "Babyn Yar," "Veechnaya Pamyat," "Changing Graves," "Before Glasnost, Oy Tovarish," and "The Gift"

C. Sonja Dunn was born in Toronto, Ontario. She received her B.A. and M.Ed. degrees from Laurentian University and the University of Toronto. A former teacher and drama consultant, she enjoyed a twenty-nine-year television career with Mid-Canada TV, a CBC and CTV affiliate that broadcast out of Sudbury, Ontario. She also wrote, produced, and hosted TV shows on the arts for Rogers Cablesystems. She is a former  president of CANSCAIP (Canadian Society of Children's Authors, Illustrators and Performers).

Sonja's stories and poems have appeared in hundreds of publications. She has presented her songs, stories, and poetry to more than a thousand audiences all over the world.

DANNY EVANISHEN

Author of "Andriy's Break"

Danny Evanishen has spent his life immersed in things Ukrainian. He was a member of Saskatoon's Ukrainian Dance Company, *Yevshan*, under the direction of Lusia Pavlychenko, and his greatest triumph was dancing for the Queen in Ottawa, Ontario, in 1967.

In addition to producing a number of books, Danny has been a teacher in Australia and New Zealand, a yacht fixer on

the Spanish island of Ibiza, a Volkswagen fixer in Africa, and a forest firefighter in the Yukon.

Always on the lookout for new or different stories, Danny urges readers to have a look at the stories in the books he has published, and then to send him their own stories. Who knows? You might end up in a book! To view a list of his publications and to contact Danny, visit www.ethnic.bc.ca

BRENDA HASIUK
Author of "It's Me, Tatia"

Brenda Hasiuk grew up in Winnipeg, Manitoba. When she is asked "What are you?" she responds, "Ukrainian—both sides."

Many of her family stories were lost as her ancestors in Canada focused on building the future. She knows that her great-grandmother Panagapko was a servant in a rich Ukrainian household, that she taught herself to read, and that she emigrated from Ukraine while she was still a teenager.

No one's sure anymore when her great-grandmother Bozohora came to Canada, or where from exactly, but she's said to have read tea leaves regularly and to have liked expensive hats.

Brenda visited Ukraine with her dance troupe in 1989, the year the Berlin Wall fell. Because neither Brenda nor her anglophone husband speaks Ukrainian, they had to rely on the kindness and patience of all they met when she visited Ukraine again in 2000. The region, its people, and the immigrant experience feature strongly in Brenda's writing.

Brenda's award-winning short fiction has appeared in a number of literary journals, including *The Malahat Review*, *Prism International*, *The New Quarterly*, and *Prairie Fire*, as well as in *Up All Night*, an anthology of stories for young people. Her first novel, *Where the Rocks Say Your Name...*, will be published by Thistledown Press in the fall of 2006.

She currently lives and writes in Winnipeg with her husband, children's author Duncan Thornton, and their baby son, Sebastian.

PAULETTE MACQUARRIE
Author of "Christmas Missed"

Paulette MacQuarrie's grandparents arrived in Canada in the early 1900s. They homesteaded as children and young adults in the Arran/Pelly area in northeastern Saskatchewan, and Paulette spent the early years of her life there. After graduating from high school in Yorkton, Saskatchewan, she lived in Winnipeg, Manitoba, for thirteen years before she and her husband moved to Vancouver, British Columbia, in 1988. As a child, Paulette was an avid reader. Her parents used to joke that the house would burn down before she'd put down the book she was reading.

Paulette began writing in 1987 while she was working for Canadian Airlines and attending the University of Manitoba part-time. She was encouraged to write by her University of

Manitoba English professor, Robin Hoople, and to write on Ukrainian themes by the then-head of the Slavic Department, Jaroslav Rozumnij. Her first newspaper article made the front page of a community newspaper in Winnipeg. In 1995, she left her airline career to launch a freelance business in writing, editing, and desktop publishing. Her work since has included ghost writing for corporate executives, project management for websites and print publications, and writing and editing website and print copy for businesses and non-profit organizations. Paulette also produces a Ukrainian music radio program that targets "born-again" Ukrainians, like herself. She is concerned with the preservation of the Ukrainian language and culture, which was all but lost in the days before it was acceptable to be ethnic.

LINDA MIKOLAYENKO
Author of "Spring Harvest" and "A Song for Kataryna"

Linda Mikolayenko is a freelance writer, broadcaster, and storyteller. She grew up in a family of seven children, on a farm near Ethelbert, Manitoba. Her educational background began with eight years in a one-room country school and developed to include a Master's degree in Human Resource Development. She has had an interesting and varied career with the Public Service of Canada.

As a child, Linda spent many hours listening to her parents' stories of life, both in Ukraine and on the Canadian prairies. It wasn't until after her own children were born, however, that she realized she wanted to share the stories of her heritage with others.

Her writing has appeared in publications such as *Reader's Digest* and *The Globe and Mail*, and has been broadcast on CBC Radio. She also has a passion for the oral tradition, and she tells folk tales and legends at schools, libraries, and festivals across the country. In 2004, Linda was selected to represent Storytellers of Canada/Conteurs du Canada during Canadian Children's Book Week.

Linda presently lives in Air Ronge, Saskatchewan, with her husband, Doug Bagwell, and their sons, Stephen and David. Her website is www.LindatheStoryteller.ca

KIM PAWLIW
Author of "Tribute to My Grandmother"

Kim Pawliw is a student at Mitchell-Montcalm high school in Sherbrooke, Quebec. She is in the school's program which puts emphasis on arts and culture. She was very close to her grandmother and was saddened to hear the story of how her own Baba was sent to an internment camp when only a child. Her affection for her grandmother motivated her to enter the Mathieu Da Costa contest, for which her story and poem received an honorable mention.

Kim likes to travel and she has visited every region of Canada. She enjoys bicycling, nature watching, drawing, writing stories, playing guitar, listening to music, and hanging out with her friends. Her favorite foods are perogies and homemade borscht. She has a black-and-white cat whose name is Pavlova.

STEFAN PETELYCKY
Author of "Auschwitz: Many Circles of Hell"

Stefan Petelycky is a retired aircraft mechanic and was a founding member of the World League of Ukrainian Political Prisoners. Since 1990, he has overseen the preparation and delivery of nineteen containers of medical equipment and other humanitarian relief supplies from Canada to Ukraine. He has also been active in the B.C. Provincial Council of the Ukrainian Canadian Congress, the Ukrainian Catholic Eparchy of British Columbia, Ukrainian Canadian Social Services, and the Ukrainian Canadian Civil Liberties Association. He was an election observer in Ukraine in 1995, 2004, and in 2006. He lives in Richmond, British Columbia, with his wife, Sofia.

OLGA PRYCHODKO
Author of "A Home of Her Own"

Olga Prychodko (whose maiden name was Harasimiw, and during her first marriage took the name Nimchuk) was a community leader, editor, author, and family matriarch. She died of natural causes on November 3, 2004, aged ninety-one years.

Olga was born in 1913. She lived in a sod house in the woods of north-central Alberta, near the North Saskatchewan River. Her father, Andriy Harasimiw, arrived in Canada in the spring of 1910. He was from Galicia in Ukraine and was one of the "men in sheepskin coats" who had been enticed by the Canadian government's promise of free land in exchange for establishing a homestead in the western Canadian wilderness. His young fiancée, Emilia Makar, followed him in the summer of 1912. Olga was born less than a year later.

Olga's father was one of the few literate settlers at the time. With books and subscriptions to progressive Ukrainian-language papers, the Harasimiw home became a gathering spot for neighbors to hear the latest news and to discuss current world affairs. It was in this literate home environment that Olga first experienced the thrill of the written word and developed her lifelong love of learning. She had been taught by her father since she was four years old and excelled as a student in the one-room schoolhouse she attended when she was seven. Olga dreamed of higher education.

In 1929, the year of the stock market crash, Olga was sixteen. Although they were very poor, her father found enough cash to billet Olga at a convent in Edmonton, Alberta, so that she could attend high school. Her dream appeared to have come true. But the Great Depression deepened and funds ran out. Olga tried to find work to stay on and continue her studies, but she was unable to do so. While it was a bitter disappointment for her to have to abandon her formal studies, she never abandoned her love of learning. She pursued learning throughout her life, and instilled her love of it in her four children and eleven grandchildren, all of whom went on to graduate from university.

Following World War II, Olga moved to Toronto, Ontario, where she was a Ukrainian community organizer. She also played a prominent role as an editor and translator. She worked on ten books and over 150 articles in the service of other Ukrainian writers and academics who had escaped Stalin's regime.

Olga set down an account of her richly lived life in her own book, *Waskatenau Girl.* It was published privately by her family on the occasion of her ninetieth birthday.

MARSHA FORCHUK SKRYPUCH
Author of "The Rings" and "The Red Boots"

Marsha Forchuk Skrypuch was born and raised in Brantford, Ontario. She knew she wanted to be a writer ever since grade four, when she read *Oliver Twist.* All she knew about Ukraine or Ukrainians was what her father had told her, until she went to university. She studied English Literature at the University of Western Ontario. While she was there, she met many members of the Ukrainian students' club. She began attending *zabavas.* She even met her husband, Orest, at a Valentine *zabava,* the first and only one he ever attended. Despite having had two different Ukrainian-language tutors as an adult, Marsha still struggles with the language. Her Master's degree in Library Science has helped her to research her subjects.

Marsha is the author of seven books for children and young adults: *Silver Threads, The Best Gifts, The Hunger, Enough, Hope's War, Nobody's Child,* and *Aram's Choice.*